Dancing with Fire

A Hal Westwood Restoration Mystery

EARLY SUMMER 1665

by Jemima Norton

TUDOR GATE PRESS

LARGE PRINT EDITION

ISBN: 0-9740949-3-5

Large Print Edition

You'll find information on the other books in this series at:
www.halwestwood.com

For ordering information visit:
www.tudorgatepress.com

This book is dedicated to:

Anne

Dancing With Fire

EARLY SUMMER 1665

Name	Age	Description
Hal Westwood	25	*Justice of the Peace*
Libby Westwood	23	*Hal's wife, Justin's sister*
Justin Danvers	22	*Lawer Hal's brother-in-law*
Susanna Blackwell	35	*Inn Keeper*
Adam Blackwell	25	*her step-son*
Edmund Benton	71	*Master Maltster*
Sophia Redcroft	18	*his Ward*
Hannah Nichols	deceased	*sister to Master Benton*
Robin Tripp	deceased	*Benton's apprentice*
Eunice Latham	38	*widowed cousin of Libby*
Dorothy Palmer	58	*kin of Mater Benton*
Guy Armstrong	28	*brother-in law to Hal*
Mary Armstrong	26	*Hal's elder sister; Guy's wife*
Cecily Armstrong	16	*Ned's betrothed, sister to Guy*
Ned Westwood	19	*Hal's brother*
Giles Durward	27	*kin of Guy Armstrong*
Jasper Durward	21	*kin of Guy Armstrong*
Denton	30	*Durward servant*

Hetta Westwood	14	*Hal's sister*
Will Shearsby	16	*Hetta's betrothed*
Bess Danvers	20	*Hal's sister*
Harry Westwood	3	*Hal & Libby's son*
Baby Francis		*Hal & Libby's son*
Margery Kingscott	60	*Hal's aunt*
Katherine Westwood	39	*Hal's aunt*
Jane Carver	22	*Hal's sister*
Jonas Capel	56	*lawyer of Chawcester*
Master Cresswell	52	*apothecary of Chawcester*
Doctor Phillipe Douay	35	*physician of Chawcester*
Wat Rose	29	*Fire dancer & baker*
Sam Hedges	38	*Fire dancer & tailor*
Will Greenway	25	*Fire dancer & cooper*
Sally Rose	23	*wife of Wat*
Owen		*boatman on the river*
Alderman Chegleigh		*Alderman*
Mayor Pegham		*Mayor of Chawcester*

Glossary

OED- Oxford English Dictionary

BD Brewer's Dictionary of Phrase & Fable

aldermen   a municipal officer ranking next to the mayor,

ale draper   an ale-house keeper,   *OED OE*

apoplexy   disabled by a stroke,   *OED ME*

apprentice/'prentice   a man of a craft, one who is bound by a legal agreement to serve an employer for a period of years to learn a trade, *OED ME*

Bacchanalia   drunken revelry; an orgy,   *OED 1633*

bagatelle   a trifle, a thing of no importance,   *OED 1645*

Beltane   the first day of May, the old May Day, when bonfires were kindled,   *OED ME*

butts   a mark, or mound, for archery practice,   *OED ME*

byword   a person or thing which has become proverbial as an object of contempt or scorn,   *OED 1535*

Castlemaine	the Duchess of Castlemaine, Barbara Villiers, mistress of Charles II
choleric disposition	Medieval, having choler as a predominant humour, irascible and passionate, *OED 1583*
cockscomb	a conceited fool, *OED 1654*
cupidity	inordinate desire to appropriate wealth or possessions, *OED ME*
cupping	operation of drawing blood into a cup as a remedy, *OED 1591*
cut-purses	one who cuts purses from a girdle or belt, hence a thief, *OED ME*
Dissenter	one who dissents in matters of religious belief or worship, *OED 1639*
Dogberry	a slow-thinking constable in Shakespeare's *Much Ado About Nothing*, *OED 16TH CENTURY*
Dutch courage	the courage exerted by drink, the Dutch were considered heavy drinkers, *BD 17TH CENTURY*

Glossary

Evensong	evening prayers of the Church of England, post-reformation, *OED 16-17TH CENTURY*
feint	a feigned, or false, attack, *OED ME*
green sickness	an anaemic disease which affected the young, giving a pale greenish complexion, *OED 1583*
groat	a coin worth fourpence, the groat went out of circulation in 1662, *OED ME*
half-timbered	a building formed of timber studding and plaster infilling, *OED*
happen	perhaps
hemlock	a poisonous plant with finely-divided leaves and small white flowers, used as a powerful sedative, *OED 1601*
horse coper	a horse dealer
hoyden	a rude, ill-bred girl, *OED 1593*
"in his cups"	said of a drunk

in his own tap	to furnish a cask with a tap for serving ale, hence, colloquially, the room in which it is served, *OED OE*
jade	a term of reprobation for a woman, *OED 1590*
jettied/jetty:	a projecting part of a building, *OED 17TH C*
jointure:	a sole estate limited to a wife, to take effect on the death of a husband, *OED 1451*
journeyman	one who, having served his apprenticeship to a trade, is qualified to work for days wages, *OED 1424*
lych-gate	the roofed gateway to a church, *OED 1482*
malady	sickness, ill-health, something which calls for a remedy, *OED ME*
malt	barley or grain prepared for brewing by steeping, germinating, and kiln-drying, *OED ME*
maltster	one whose occupation to make malt, *OED ME*

May-game	the merrymakings associated with the first of May, *OED 1549*
megrims	a nervous or sick headache, *OED 1595*
missle	misty drizzle
Noll	nickname for Oliver Cromwell, Lord Protector of the Common-weath
noon-piece	short for a piece of bread, collo-quialism, *OED ME*
pall	a cloth of black, purple or white velvet spread over a coffin, *OED 1440*
pate	crown of the head, or skull, *OED ME*
physic/physicking	medicine, a cathartic or purge, *OED ME*
pillion	to ride behind another on a horse, *OED 1503*
poppy seed drops	the plant or its extract used in pharmacy, *OED 1604*

rapine	acts of violent robbery or pillage, *OED ME*
rigor	numbness, stiffness of body, especially following death, *OED ME*
Robin Goodfellow	a sportive, capricious, elf or goblin, believed to haunt the countryside, *OED 1531*
Roundhead	one who sided with Parliament in the English Civil War
scurvy	sorry, worthless, contemptible, *OED 1579*
sen'night	seven nights, a week
Shrovetide	the period compromising Quinquagesima Sunday and the two following days, *OED ME*
simples	a medicine composed of only one ingredient, and hence a plant employed for such purposes, *OED 1560*
sovereign remedy	the best, most expensive, potion for the purpose

stave	thin, narrow shaped pieces of wood, which when placed collectively side by side and hooped, will form a cask or barrell, *OED ME*
stripling	a youth, one just passing from boyhood to manhood, *OED ME*
the Common	a tract of pastureland held in joint occupation by the community, *OED 1663*
the Commonwealth	the Republican government in England between 1649-1660
the Watch	a body of men who patrolled and guarded the streets of a town and proclaimed the hour, *OED 1593*
unchancy	ill-omened, ill-fated, unfortunate, *OED 1533*
virago	a bold, impudent woman, a termagant, a scold, *OED ME*

English Legal Terms

Act of Indemnity: the act that facilitated the return of Charles II and decided how property was to be divided amongst Royalists and Parliamentarians

Assizes: the sessions held periodically in each county of England for the purpose for administering Civil and Criminal justice by judges acting under certain special permissions, *OED ME*

Justice: a colloquial term for Justice of the Peace, an inferior magistrate appointed to preserve the peace in county, town, or other district, and to discharge other local magisterial functions, *OED ME*

Petty sessions: a court of three Justices of the Peace who dispensed summary justice

Quarter sessions: a court to hear crimes which could not be tried summarily by Justices of the Peace. Made up of two or more Justices of the Peace and a chairman who sat with a jury. Did not have jurisdiction to hear most serious crimes or those which could be punished by capital punishment

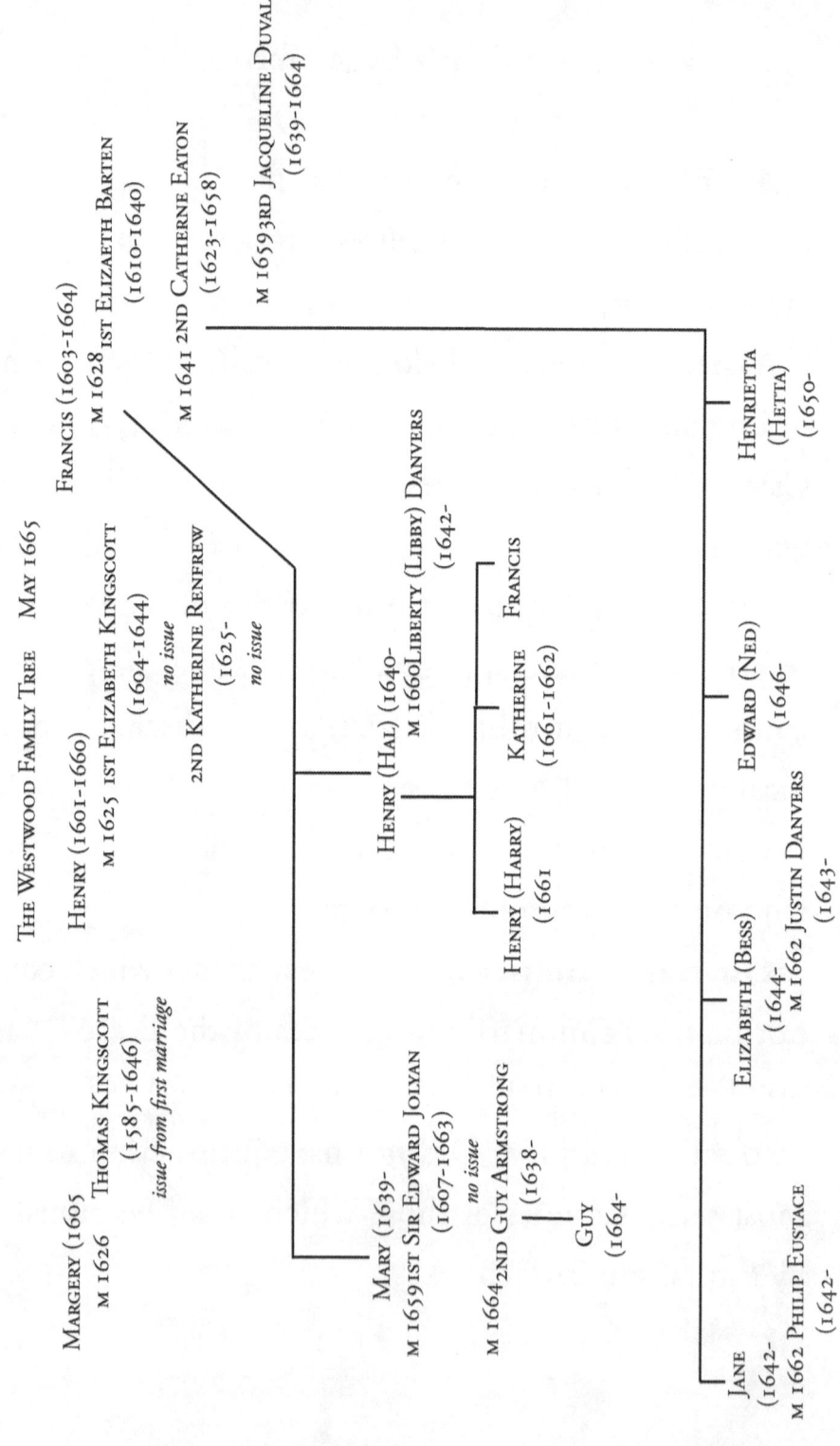

The Westwood Family Tree   May 1665

THE HAL WESTWOOD RESTORATION MYSTERY SERIES

❧

BOOK 1

A Flutter in the Dovecote
Summer 1660

BOOK 2

A Storm in the Wassail Bowl
Christmas 1663

BOOK 3

A Trip to Jericho
Summer 1664

(Refresh your memory by reading the last chapter of
the previous book beginning on page 306)

BOOK 4

Dancing With Fire
Summer 1665

Enjoy the first chapter in the next book
in the Hal Westwood series,
which starts at the end of this book on page 310

BOOK 5

Calling the Kettle Black
Autumn 1665

Chapter One

The face of the blonde giant of an innkeeper changed at the question. "Sir Henry Westwood?" he repeated the words, and if he didn't spit, the sense of it was in the tone of his voice. "Yes, he's here."

"Good, then I shall require lodgings, too," said Justin Danvers. "And a hot supper, if you'll be so good."

"'Tis latish!" muttered the innkeeper sullenly.

"Indeed it is," agreed Justin. "I've travelled many miles to get here, I am weary and I'd appreciate a hot meal at once."

"At once, your honour," an older woman said, as she came hurrying to them. She cast the innkeeper a frowning look and continued: "I've a rabbit pie as will go down a treat, aye, and just the last portion of a baron of beef that Sir Henry himself complimented me upon! Will your honour be a friend of Sir Henry?"

"I am married to his sister," replied Justin, as the inn-keeper returned to serving ale with sour grace.

"Then I've no doubt he'll be glad to see you, for a man powerful for his family, they do say Sir Henry be! Will you be pleased to follow me, Mr—"

"Danvers," he replied. "Justin Danvers."

"I'll put you up here, near Sir Henry." She led the way up a creaking set of stairs and along a low-beamed corridor. "Sir Henry being Justice at the Sessions, he has his own private parlour. Alas, I have only the one to offer, your honour."

"No matter," said Justin pleasantly, following her over the threshold, down two steps into another low room with a large casement window. He cast his hat and gloves to the comfortable-looking bed, noting the linen looked spotless. "Someone will bring up my bags?"

"At once, your honour, and if you are wanting to visit Sir Henry, I could serve your supper in his parlour, sir. You'll find it a deal more comfortable than the dining parlour, which is overfull, it being market day."

"Was it market day?" Justin asked. "Yes, I never thought, but thank you, Mistress—?"

"Blackwell, your honour," she replied with a dimpled smile and a curtsey. "Susanna Blackwell."

"Thank you, Mistress Blackwell, I'll do just that," he replied, realising that she wasn't in fact much older than her husband.

She bustled away, whilst Justin, staying only to wash off the dust of the road, walked along the corridor and down two steps to the private parlour. He entered on command and paused in the doorway, rapidly scanning his brother-in-law's face in the candlelight for any confirmation of his sister's fears.

"Justin?" Hal said blankly. "What do you—" Then in quick fear, he added: "Libby—the children?"

"All alive and well, not three hours since," he replied swiftly. "Especially the baby, young Francis. By heavens, what a pair of lungs! It seemed my lord was ahungered and would not wait. He is most definitely your father again, Hal."

Hal's face, relieved of care, relaxed into a slight smile. "Yes, he is, isn't he," he agreed. "And doesn't he like the admiration too?"

"I'd have not thought it possible in one but a month old, but yes," Justin agreed with a smile. "So I've left my brood with Libby and Jane for a few days," he added, "and thought to come to join you here."

Hal's handsome face took on a sardonic look. "By

whose order?" he enquired tartly.

"No order," replied Justin, with an air of innocence. "*'But longen folk to go on pilgrimages in April,'* you know, and I've had word through my cousin Eunice about a possible client who feels he has a matter of some concern to put before me. So I thought, why not? Hal can bear the company, I am sure."

"Yes, you and your sister are so very transparent," Hal replied with a satirical glance. "I know she's sent you to watch over me."

"Are you a child, then, to need watching?" Justin asked mildly.

"No indeed!" he retorted robustly. "But I know Libby when she gets herself into one of her fusses."

Justin smiled innocently. "Hal, in truth, I had to come to Chawcester, and the Greyhound is the best inn."

"Run by the surliest innkeeper," replied Hal.

"Yes indeed," laughed Justin. "What a welcome! How does he get trade? But of course, his wife is very comely."

"Not his wife, his stepmother," replied Hal. "Mistress Blackwell was married to his father, a ruined King's man, or so she tells me, who lost vast estates in the last war. Did not everyone? It would seem the Greyhound Inn was all that remained to them. I am given to understand that Master Blackwell senior drunk himself into oblivion fairly quickly, but his son has decided to hold a grudge against the world."

"The whole world, or just you personally?" Justin asked smiling.

"I am doubly in his bad books, for I sent a friend of his off to the Assizes yesterday, where I devoutly trust he'll be transported to the colonies, and bad luck to them as far as I can see," he replied, with a return to his former gloom.

"May I help myself to a cup of your wine?" Justin asked as he darted him a sharp glance.

"Do and be welcome," he replied, drinking off his own.

"I've further imposed upon your good nature, by telling Mistress Blackwell to serve me my supper here," Justin continued, pouring wine for them both.

Hal shrugged his acceptance, and returned to his chair, yawning prodigiously. "Bess is well?" He asked after a space. "And the baby?"

"Both are very well," he replied. "I'd not have left them else, but we think Bess is with child again, so we thought a little country air would be best for them both, through the heat of the summer. There are cases of plague in Adamsholme."

"Are there?" Hal asked sharply. "That's bad news. You must take care upon your return, Justin, I know there are always a few cases, but I live in dread of a bad attack!"

"I think we all do," agreed Justin. "And we were lucky last summer. No more than twenty taken in all, Hal. I must admit, I was never more thankful than that you made us stay at Westwood, and that you got us from London, for there were a good few cases there, as ever. Both Jack Steene and Will Johnson were killed you know, and their clerk, not to mention the people in Rankin's Court."

"Yes, it must have been a prime area," agreed Hal. "But many towns and villages suffer every year. We were lucky at Westwood."

"Especially lucky, when you consider Hughes's man, Hoskins, died not a month after he visited us," said Justin.

"Yes," agreed Hal, his thoughts going back to the previous summer. "Yes, very lucky in many ways, even poor Will survived with Hetta's nursing, though he is but a shadow of his former self."

"He's gaining ground," soothed Justin. "He'll do better now the warm weather is here. Not much of a start to married life for poor Hetta, though. Little more than a month a bride and her groom at death's door."

"Not to mention Will's mother going as she did within a few hours," said Hal. "Such grief for the poor lad."

"Yet a blessing in some ways for Hetta, you can't deny," said Justin. "It would have been a difficult life with Mistress Shearsby as her mother-in-law."

"Yes, especially after the scandal broke about Eustace's death," said Hal. "I must say, Isaac Hughes stood by us in a magnificent manner."

"Mmn," said Justin. "He's improved enormously since he doesn't personally hold you and I responsible for every murder locally."

Hal chuckled as a knock came upon the door. "Ah, Mistress Blackwell, is that my brother's supper? He is obliged to you," he said, the laughter still in his voice.

"Nay then, your honour, I'm obliged to him," she replied, her eyes bright. "Ah, but his coming has banished your melancholy, and for that you must be doubly thankful! Such a time as he's been having at the Sessions, your honour," she continued, turning to Justin. "Such dreadful long pleas, and his honour forced to sit best part of the day, listening to a lot of lies told by lawyers."

"Nay, you must not say so," said Hal gently. "Lies they are not, merely differing versions of the truth. Especially you must not say so, before this gentleman, for he, too, is a lawyer."

"Nay, then!" she cried indignantly. "As if we've not enough of these rascals of our own, without more coming. For that Jonas Capel, now, he's a rogue as anyone who lives in Chawcester will tell you."

"No ma'am, you must not tell me," Hal replied patiently.

"I assure you, Mistress Blackwell, I've been sent for," said Justin, in some amusement, hungrily attacking his supper. "By a Master Benton, a Maltster?"

"Edmund Benton has sent for you?" the woman cried, opening her deep blue eyes wide.

"Well," amended Justin. "My cousin, Eunice Latham, recommended me to her sister-in-law, Dorothy Palmer, and is not Master Benton her brother?"

"Only by marriage," she replied, but she was obviously impressed by this pedigree. "Oh aye, I never said Edmund Benton wasn't well-connected. That's what makes it all the more shocking, I suppose."

"Shocking?" said Hal, succumbing to her lure.

"It'll be about the lad, I suppose," she continued, and a faint smile curved her lips, for she'd been trying to remove the blank look from her important visitor's eyes for the last few days. Why, she didn't know, but that he stirred something within her. Yes, he was handsome, very handsome, but it was more than that. The air of melancholy that hung about him had wrung her heart many a time, bringing out all her motherly instincts. "Poor thing! Ah, but he was a golden lad, if you know what I mean."

"Was?" said Hal.

"An apprentice of Mr Benton was killed last month," said Justin. "Robin Tripp, his name was, just finished his time—and was universally popular."

"Not universally so," replied Hal dryly.

"Well, perhaps not," agreed Justin. "Although it may only have been an accident."

"Pooh, that was no accident," Mistress Blackwell replied tartly. "Robin were the best fire dancer we've ever seen! This were the third year that he leapt the flames at Beltane for luck, and none able to go higher."

"Leapt the flames for luck?" Hal repeated the words incredulously.

"'Tis a custom, Hal, going back to ancient times, when the young lad was indeed a sacrifice to the forthcoming season," explained Justin.

"As it would appear this poor fellow was," said Hal in disgust. "I trust the town does well out of his blood."

"Nay then, Sir Henry, 'tis nowt but a bit of fun on a fair day," she cried, sensing his disapproval. "The local lads train for it, they do for weeks, and generally, it be safer than football that they play at Chipping Barbury on Easter Day! Over in Chipping Barbury there is always a death, at least, and I don't know how many broken heads besides."

"These sports and games take place in most towns and villages at this time of the year, Hal," said Justin in explanation, as Hal looked appalled at this description. "Did they not do a like thing in France when you were there?"

"Not that I recall," he replied frowning. "But then we were seldom in one place for any length of time. I certainly don't recall them occurring in England, when I was a child."

"They died out a lot in the war," said the landlady preparing to leave. "I guess there were enough killing to satisfy the blood-lust of most men then."

"She's right," said Hal thoughtfully, as she closed the door behind herself. "That's what it amounts to, isn't it?"

"I don't know until I've investigated it," said Justin. "I shall begin by interviewing Master Benton tomorrow. Have you seen much of Mary and Guy?"

"No," he replied. "I've been too busy and they have been taken up with these cousins of Guy's, who are staying with them." He grinned suddenly. "I gather Guy's not best pleased with the elder of them, it seems he has some land in Hereford, and Guy and Mary make a convenient stopping off place in his journey. Guy said to me, that he never knew he had cousins from Hampshire until he made a fortune, now suddenly he has a whole host of kin there."

Justin smiled faintly. "Is Ned still with them?"

"Aye, and still bemoaning fate and his put off marriage," Hal agreed.

"Both him and Ambrose," said Justin. "He wrote to me only last week saying that he thought this year would never be done with, but I wrote saying that by the time he'd eaten his dinners at the Inns and qualified enough to help me, it would almost be next January." He paused, choosing his words carefully. "That's when you agreed upon for the weddings, isn't it?"

"Well, my father will only have been dead just over the year, but Ned insists he won't wait a day longer," replied Hal sourly.

"Well, Ned is very much in love," said Justin gently.

"Aye, but… Oh well, there's no point in going over it again. Tell me instead about this boy Robin Tripp, do they suspect foul play?"

"Presumably so, or I'd not have been sent for," Justin replied. "I know little more than the barest facts, but if you care to accompany me tomorrow, perhaps we can discover more. You don't sit again until Monday, do you?"

"No, no, I don't," he said thoughtfully. "And yes, it might be pleasant to bend my mind about different problems. I'll gladly accompany you tomorrow to visit your worthy Maltster."

❧

Chapter Two

"Where are they off to?" asked Adam Blackwell sharply, as Hal and Justin left the inn. The two men crossed to the shady side of the narrow street and walked past the half-timbered jettied houses that lined it.

"To see Master Benton," replied Susanna as she stood in the gateway of the yard, watching them go. She surveyed Hal's broad back, clothed in an immaculately fitting blue coat with immense satisfaction. "It would seem he's sent for the other one, the lawyer, Mr Danvers."

"Lawyer pshaw!" he said sourly. He glanced to the comely woman, irritation writ on his own handsome face. "And I see you've been taken in by the pretty face and fancy manners yet again," he added.

"'Tis nice to be in company with a gentleman again," she agreed, "rather than a surly bear."

"I fit myself for the company I keep," he snapped.

"Where would long speeches and French manners get me, with a crowd of drunken farmers on market day?"

"Happen, if you recollect your breeding, you'd not need to be serving drunken farmers on market day," she retorted. "This is the best inn in town. We should only deal with the carriage trade."

"Carriage trade!" he repeated with a sneer. "What carriage trade?"

"The trade that stops at the Bell by the Abbey because your sour manners have chased them away," she replied sweetly.

"The Bell is on the London Road," he cried indignantly. "Not many coachmen want to turn by the Cross if they are going to London."

"Certainly not to be met by your sour looks," she agreed, turning away as her guests disappeared from view in the bustle of the High Street.

"What does Master Benton want with them anyway?" he asked, unwilling to continue an argument he was clearly losing.

"He didn't actually say," she replied, reviewing the matter. "I assumed it was because of poor Robin Tripp."

"Oh him!" he replied dismissively. His thoughts ran off at a tangent to Sophia Redcroft. Then, as he realised the implication, "Why for?"

"I don't know, but Sir Henry suggested foul play," she said with a sigh. "He was shocked by the manner of the lad's death. Sir Henry spent his youth in France, you know, on account of the war and so hadn't heard of such customs."

"Aye, so I've heard," snapped Adam. "One of Dame Fortune's chosen ones isn't he, Sir Henry Westwood?" He continued. "His father was for the King, and they, like so many, were totally ruined. Then, as they faced a future as bleak as most of us, what happened? Up came an uncle, who husbanded his money through the war offering to make him his heir if he'll marry an heiress. Which, of course, he does. His uncle dies promptly, leaving him his estates, and Master Henry Westwood is set up for life, only needing the title his father got by dubious means to complete the transformation."

"Poor Adam," she remarked kindly. "It was a great shame you've lost everything, but it does no good to repine on it. Elmley Park is sold again, you know, and even if you could have married Sophia Redcroft, you'd have needed Master Benton's money to purchase it, and he was set against you." She sighed and crossed to pat his massive shoulders. "It does seem hard when one is the favoured of fortune, and the other takes all the knocks, but it does no good to be bitter about it."

"The Westwoods were nothing, you know," he cried, by no means mollified by her words. "They were no better than the rest of us, but Francis Westwood was a scurvy fellow, with his fingers in plots and such, and for his son to sentence poor Jack to the Assizes like that—"

"But Jack had turned highwayman, Adam," she cried, interrupting. "I know he used to be your groom, but to turn to robbery and kill a man, I think he'll be lucky to escape with his life! Indeed, if Jonas Capel hadn't said how he'd fought for the King, and Sir Henry not agreed to recommend transportation to America, I don't doubt he would hang!"

"Jonas Capel!" The Innkeeper snarled. "Jack was worth three of that scurvy knave! If only he'd come to me, instead of taking to the road."

"He'd got past earning an honest penny, Adam," she said patiently. "You know he had. He'd have surely stolen from us, as he had from travellers, and who's to know whether or not he'd have killed one of us, too."

"Aye, who's to say?" he agreed sharply. "Who is to say that he mayn't have been a good and honest worker!"

"Well, he's got a chance now," she returned tartly.

"If Sir Henry's words have any effect, happen he'll be transported. He can work his sentence, and then turn his hand to carving his life in the colonies."

"If Sir Henry Westwood has an ounce of influence at the Assizes! If Jack survives the voyage! If he outlives his sentence! If he's not an old man at the end of it!" Adam retorted, stumping off and back into the inn.

Susanna Blackwell shrugged her plump shoulders and, bethinking her of her errands, stepped out into the street on her way to the quayside and the fishmongers.

❧

Hal and Justin, meanwhile, had entered the commodious town house of one of the leading citizens of Chawcester and been shown up a very handsome staircase to a panelled parlour, which overlooked a small garden backing on to the river.

"A wealthy man," Hal remarked, noting tall bookcases with volumes safe behind glass.

"Aye," agreed Justin. "He's made his fortune from roasting malt, but according to my Cousin Eunice, that's not his only source of income. He owns boats on the river, a mill upstream and enough land under plough to keep both the mill and boats busy."

"Yet not an uncultured man," said Hal, his eyes travelling about the apartment, which was well-furnished, but with great taste and little show.

"Indeed a veritable paragon, not the common run of Maltster as popular imagination would have him," said Justin. "He's been Mayor three times, and is not only well-respected, but I gather, he is affectionately held by most townsfolk. Yet, he has no chick, nor child, to leave his considerable fortune to."

"What, none?" Hal asked, amazed.

"His only son was killed at Marston Moor," said Justin. "He did remarry, but his second wife followed her child to the grave. His heiress is the granddaughter of an old companion-at-arms, a Mistress Sophia Redcroft. He took her into his house when her father died during the Commonwealth. He was one of these fanatical preachers who spent many months each year in prison, until his health broke down."

"I see you've done your research well," Hal smiled. "Is this heiress young and pretty?"

"Are they not all?" Justin retorted. "Eighteen years old is Mistress Sophia, and possessed, so our landlady says, of a pair of violet eyes."

"And the foulest temper ever vented on a poor old

man," said their host entering the parlour.

Hal, assessing the man as wine was offered, thought him neither poor nor old. Master Benton was plainly a good age, in his late sixties at a guess, but so hale and hearty-looking, in spite of his white hair and beard, and with such an upright bearing that he might be taken for considerably younger.

"So, Mr Danvers, you are interested in my puzzle," he remarked, once they'd all been served and the initial discussion of local topics and the weather dealt with.

"Intrigued," agreed Justin. "My Cousin Eunice was rather insistent I came, if only to reassure you of no foul play."

"Oh, there was foul play, depend upon it," the older man replied swiftly. "A promising young lad, cut down like that." He hesitated, shaking his head, and then added: "My own boy was killed at no age, slaughtered before my eyes, by a rascally cur of a Roundhead. I thought at that time I'd never love another like my boy, but young Robin—" He shook his head again. "He was no kin of mine, but a lad I took on as an apprentice. I have taken on an apprentice every year since the end of the war. Robin wasn't out of the common way to look at, pleasing, aye, with his tightly-curling hair and bright eyes, especially for a lad. He was small for his age at the beginning, but he had one of those sweet, loving natures, so that before I knew it, I loved him like a son."

Hal warmed to the man with his frank manner. "Did everybody find him equally lovable, Master Benton?" he asked astutely.

"Aye, they did, for the most part," said the old man quickly. "There were few that could withstand his charm. Robin Goodfellow I used to call him, for he had his naughty side too, but nothing malicious, you understand, more mischief."

"But someone didn't care for him," Justin suggested, seeing a reminiscent gleam in the old man's eye, and having no desire to get lost in a font of fond memories.

"Only those with crabbed natures or jealous streaks," sighed the old man. "My sister Hannah, rest her soul, never cared for him. I confess she was on occasion the target of his japes, but then if she hadn't been such a cheerless soul…"

"When did your sister die?" asked Justin swiftly.

"Oh, last August, of the fever, poor soul," replied the Maltster. "She was a great one for charitable works. Her husband had been a minister, before he was took, and she saw it as her Christian duty to take alms to the poor, and to scold them back to the path of righteousness. Unfortunately, she took the sickness from some of the folk in the back alleys and died within three days. Robin helped me to nurse her."

"Were you both not afraid?" asked Hal curiously.

"At my age, one has little fear of death," replied the old man. "One accepts death is lingering at hand, the guise he takes cannot matter. Robin said if the Lord was taking people as good as Mistress Nichols, he'd have to be prepared to meet his Maker."

"He sounds too good be true," said Hal thoughtfully.

"Nay, then, to report it so sounds trite," replied Master Benton. "He was a normal, healthy lad too, but loveable."

"You'd planned a match between him and your ward, Mistress Sophia Redcroft?" asked Justin, who'd begun to take notes.

"Aye," agreed the man, settling more comfortably into his chair. "I intended to leave Sophia well-provided for, but as I say, she's a will of her own, and leave her my fortune outright, I will not do."

"Were both parties happy with the match?" asked Hal.

"They could have been, given time," said Master Benton.

"Robin, as ever, saw the sense in the match. He'd become my journeyman, and so understood the business, and wasn't adverse to Sophie, for make no mistake, she is a beauty."

"And Mistress Sophia?" Justin asked.

"The wench is a fool," grumbled the old man. "She said she'd nothing against Robin, that she loved him as much as his inches. There, what do you make of that?"

"That Mistress Sophia was not inclined," Hal said with a smile. "Has she another lover?"

"No," he cried instantly. "She does not, whatever she may think! T'was Robin, or none other, as far as I was concerned."

"Let me understand you," said Justin. "As it stands, Mistress Sophia only inherits if she marries at your bidding?"

"Aye," the older man replied, folding his arms across his chest. "And I'll never consent to her wedding Adam Blackwell!"

"Adam Blackwell? He that is our host at the Greyhound?" cried Hal. "He is her lover?"

"No, I tell you, I'll not countenance it," snapped the Maltster. "She's been taken in by all his talk of being a gentleman. Some gentleman, to serve all and sundry in his own tap all day."

"It is said he lost his fortune in the war," said Justin probing gently.

"Oh aye, his family owned Elmley Park, before they sold it to pay fines," agreed the old man. "But many lost and some won in the war. 'Tis the way of the world."

"Indeed," Hal agreed, glancing in dismay to Justin, for their brother-in-law, Guy Armstrong had just bought Elmley Park at a handsome price from its former owner. Hal suddenly realised that this gave the surly young innkeeper even more cause to dislike them.

"So, in essence then, Adam Blackwell must know you'd not consent to his being the husband of your ward," said Justin.

"Aye, I told him so to his face last Shrovetide," Master Benton replied in a forthright manner. "I walked down the High Street on purpose and waylaid him in his own tavern! 'Take my ward to wife,' I said, 'and you take a pauper, so you can be poor together!'"

"Blackwell isn't poor, surely," said Hal, "he has the Greyhound, that must give him a substantial income."

"The Greyhound is Mistress Blackwell's jointure," snapped the Maltster. "She has her income first and foremost from it. Most years he barely clears his debts, but he needn't think to improve his fortune with mine. I told him that to his head, too. My hard-won money wasn't going to purchase Elmley Park back again for him. Anyway, 'tis too late now, a Bristol tradesman has bought the place."

"Guy Armstrong is a gentleman!" said Hal sharply. "He fought for the King and lost his own manor, much the same as Blackwell did. But fortune has lately favoured him; in a partnership with Mr Danvers' late father, they funded a trip to the Indies, the result of which has purchased Elmley Park for Guy and his wife, my sister."

"Then the fellow is your brother-in-law," said the older man. "Good heavens, what a small world! And he went into partnership with your father, Mr Danvers?"

"Yes," said Justin. "Although, I had quarrelled with my late father, so I didn't make the money Guy did. My sister, Mr Westwood's wife, was my father's heir."

"Only because you are so stubborn, Justin," said Hal, getting hastily to his feet. "Do you imagine either Libby or I would ever—Good heavens!" He paused at the window overlooking the garden, "I imagine this to be Mistress Sophia! You are right, sir, she is a beauty! And what is more, she plainly considers Blackwell her lover!"

"Blackwell!" the old man cried, getting to his feet. He came to stare out of the window, suppressing an oath at the sight of a lovely young lady sitting close in a shady bower with the innkeeper. Abruptly, he opened the casement and leant out precariously. "Sophie! Sophie, come here at once!" he cried angrily.

"I am busy, sir," the reply drifted up on a balmy breeze.

"At once, do you hear!" he repeated wrathfully.

A silence ensued, as the young lady flounced from sight trailed by her disconsolate lover. The old man shut the window, tutting audibly.

"'Twasn't so in my day," he muttered. "If I'd have dared speak so to one of my elders, I'd have been beaten to within an inch of my life."

"Aye sir, and the better for it," Justin agreed, looking shocked, as steps were heard outside the door.

⚜

Chapter Three

The door was opened with a snap, and one of the loveliest maids Hal had ever seen entered.

Blonde curls rippled from an ivory brow, violet eyes snapped from beneath perfectly arched eyebrows and rosy red lips were pursed petulantly. "Well sir, here I am," she cried in a scold's tone. "What will you?"

"Pray, sit, Mistress Redcroft," said Justin politely. "And answer a few of our questions, if you will be so good."

Her eyes travelled to his face, and then to Hal's, widening slightly in admiration.

"These gentlemen are here to look into Robin's death, Sophie," said Master Benton, eyeing her doubtfully.

Sophie's eyes clouded slightly and she came to take the seat Justin indicated, whilst Adam Blackwood stood awkwardly in the doorway. "Sophie, love," he stammered. "Should I not—that is—would it not be better if…"

"Oh sit do, Adam!" she said impatiently, raising her eyes to Hal and Justin in a manner which took Hal's breath away. "Well, sirs, how can I assist you?"

"You were betrothed to Master Robin Tripp?" asked Justin, as Hal seemed loath to speak.

"No, sir, I was not," she replied sharply. "Uncle Edmund, how could you tell these gentlemen such a story? I never agreed to marry Robin Tripp, never!"

"You are an unnatural child!" Master Benton cried fretfully. "I wished you to marry Robin, that should have been enough."

"Adam, you will stand my witness. I never agreed to marry, did I?" she cried, turning to him in appeal.

"That is so," he agreed reluctantly, with a depressed air. "She's never agreed to marry anyone."

"Mistress Redcroft is perhaps a little young to rush into matrimony," said Hal gently. "So, there was no formal agreement, but you were aware of your guardian's wishes?"

"Oh yes!" she agreed, with a toss of her curls. "Uncle Edmund made it plain, that if I wished to inherit his fortune, I must marry as he wills it."

"And Robin Tripp, did he will it, too?" Justin asked.

"Robin was no fool," she replied. "He could see his way to a comfortable life."

"Not with a scold for a wife, he couldn't," said Master Benton maliciously.

"I never scolded Robin. He didn't try one's patience." She glanced to Hal, her expression confiding. "Robin wasn't like that, he said he was more than happy to be wed, but he'd not press me to it, if I didn't care to. He said an unwilling wife must be the devil!"

Hal found himself drawn to both her and the young man she spoke of. "He sounds a most reasonable fellow," he agreed. "Well-liked, too, no doubt?" Then, as she nodded, he added, "yet, somebody plainly held a grudge, don't you think? Or, he'd still be alive today."

"Nay then," said Adam Blackwell, from the back of the room.

"Robin Tripp fell. He was chocked full of pride from his fire-leaping, and pride goeth before a fall!"

"'Pride goeth before destruction and a vain spirit before a fall'," Sophie corrected him, adding as Justin looked surprised, "Mistress Nichols was forever quoting scriptures at me."

"Well, then," said Adam, looking harassed. "It doesn't

make any difference, he tripped and fell into the fire. It has happened afore, 'twill happen again. 'Tis a foolish custom anyway!"

"But why should such a good, fit, young fellow fall?" Justin asked. "Did any see it, were you close at hand?"

"Nay," said Adam quickly, "I was serving ale."

"And I was with Uncle Edmund on the far side of the fire, quarrelling. He was trying to bully me into allowing him to announce my betrothal, and I was refusing."

"Who was with Robin?" Justin asked.

"Walter Rose, Sam Hedges, and Will Greenway, happen," said Adam. "They all leapt the fire, too."

"It's a local test of male strength, is it?" Hal asked, glancing at the innkeeper, who appeared much younger and uncertain in Sophie's company.

Adam shrugged. "Happen," he replied truculently.

"Yet, you do not compete?" remarked Hal, who disliked his manner more and more. "A splendid fellow like you was content to serve ale?"

Adam's eyes flashed. "'Tis beneath me to leap the flames," he said. "I'm forced to play the part of a tradesman, but I am not one of them."

"Yet, you speak like one of them," countered Hal swiftly, seeing that the innkeeper's guard was down, and hoping to get under it. Then, as Adam glared at him, he added softly, "I, too, once faced an uncertain future. My brother-in-law, here, has more recently had to take a step down in station, yet I swear to you, I'd go in rags before I spoke like an oaf."

The blue eyes flashed fire again. "If you weren't a Justice, I'd thrash you for that!" Adam cried, all his pent-up anger spilling over again.

"Don't let that stop you," cried Hal insolently, "glad to have the acrimony out in the open!"

"Hal, Hal!" Justin cried, taken aback. "A little less heat, if you please! What purpose can be served by antagonizing Mr Blackwell?"

"I thought we might get some truth," Hal replied. "Besides, I grow weary of his enmity. Does he imagine he is the only one who has had to make sacrifices since the war?"

"What sacrifices had you had to suffer?" cried Adam hotly. "You sit there, Justice of the Peace, Sir Henry Westwood, with your father's title, your rich wife, and your uncle's estate, all borrowed feathers, and lecture me on sacrifice!"

"I don't lecture anyone," said Hal, his face pale at the truth of this. "I merely say that few returning King's men have found life the bed of roses they imagined in exile. That many of them may have had to continue to adapt as they learnt abroad, if they were to survive, but most have better manners than to bemoan their fate and take their resentment out on their fellow man."

"Oh, well said, Sir Henry," cried Sophie, clapping her hands together. "Yes, exactly so! You'd be a much nicer fellow, Adam, if you'd let go your grudge against the world. If you don't have a care, you'll settle into a churlish old man before your time."

Justin, observing the innkeeper's face thought for a moment there might be murder done. Then, the innkeeper got stiffly to his feet. "In that case, ma'am, I'll take my self off, before I disgust anyone further!" he snapped, his face white with fury.

"Yes, do, there's a good fellow," she replied cheerfully. "And try to find some good humour, I vow I am weary of bad-tempered men."

"Happen, wench, you make for bad-tempered men!" exclaimed Master Benton, as Adam stormed out of the house.

"Oh, I don't think that likely, do you, gentlemen?" Sophie asked, turning with a smile to Justin.

"Do you regret Robin Tripp's death, Mistress Sophia?" he replied, wondering if she were merely a spoilt beauty

Her pretty face crumpled at once. "Oh yes," she said with patent honesty. "I didn't care to marry Robin, but he was such a good, kind fellow. 'Tis terrible to think of him snuffed out like that, and to die in such agony, too!"

"Nay, nay, lass, he weren't in pain, not at the last," said the Maltster, whose eyes had also filled with tears. "We gave him poppy seed drops to kill the worst of it. Master Cresswell was very good. If only we could have broken the fever, who knows, he might have lived."

"He didn't care to, Uncle," she replied gently, tears sliding down her cheeks now. "I could tell that, and who could blame him. He'd have been a cripple and a monster to look at! Robin, who was so light-footed and comely, a shuffling scarfaced figure for children to poke fun at? No, 'twas better this way!"

"Aye happen 'tis so," he agreed, coming to pat her shoulders. "There, there, don't cry, lass. I'm sorry if I were sharp with you, but I'm that put about by grief." He sighed and sat down. "As one gets older, one forgets a youngster's capacity for going on with life. You are right, Sophie, tears won't bring him back."

"No, uncle, but if it was foul play, I'd like to see him avenged," she replied, glancing through her tears to Justin and Hal. "What think you, gentlemen?"

"That it is early days yet, ma'am," replied Hal. "Tell me, where will we find Walter Rose, Samuel Hedges and William Greenway?"

"Sam Hedges is a dissenter, so he'll be at their meeting on the Common," said Master Benton. "They have one every Saturday, to drum up trade for Sunday."

"Will Greenway often practices at the Butts," said Sophie. "And Wat Rose will be in one of the taverns. Now, if it had been he who had fallen dancing the flames, I'd not have been surprised, for he's becoming a regular drunk."

"Aye," Master Benton nodded. "Aye, the fellow's a fool! He took to wife a veritable scold of a wench, and now flees her at the bottom of an ale pot!"

"Nay, Uncle," cried Sophie. "'Tis his fecklessness that so enrages Sally Rose! Three babies in three years, and he needs must waste his time and money in taverns! Flour going sour in the bins, and bread stale on the shelf because he is too drunk to open the shop! She was there herself yesterday, with one little one in a basket, another on the floor, and the third on her hip, selling what she'd baked, but she's not a master baker and is too weak to stand the hours. 'Tis a shame and a scandal."

"'Tis indeed," he agreed. "The town council should do something about it!"

"They have," cried Sophie, "oh aye, with a true masterstroke, they fined him! Now Sally has even less money and is reduced to baking only for her own needs, until all her debts fall due at the end of the month, then presumably, she'll beg in the streets."

"Well, 'tis not easy to see what else could be done," he replied defensively.

"They should ban the man from every ale house in town," she retorted roundly.

"You can't do that to a man," cried the Maltster shocked. "'Tis his right to take a drink of ale."

"Is it his right to ruin his business and starve his children," Sophie cried, incensed, "with none of you other men even putting out a hand to stay him?"

"Well, well, you females don't understand business," he replied evading this question. "'Tis not a matter so easily settled."

"Well, of course it is," she cried angrily. "Don't pat my head and tell me to run away and play! I am neither a child nor a fool."

"Nay, you are fast becoming a scold!" he snapped.

"Have you ever noticed, gentlemen, how it is that a female who speaks the truth is a scold?" Sophie cried scornfully, turning her appeal to the visitors.

Hal, who'd been enjoying the exchange, hid a smile, saying pointedly: "I rather think, Mistress Sophia, 'tis the manner of your delivery that does that. To stand thus, arms akimbo, berating a man who advances a fair and just argument, will always procure for you the same epithet!"

He met her scorching glare without turning a hair. "In future, if you could but remember to lower your tone to a small voice of calm, and adjust your stance to one of meek propriety, most men would no longer be frightened by your truth! Granted, it would still be the same truth, but it would get a fairer hearing, and we may find it more palatable."

"So you'd have me dissemble and flatter your vanity?" she cried, her eyes flashing contempt as she spoke.

"I would say that rather depends upon whether you are concerned more with righting the wrongs of your contemporary, Mrs Rose, or with your personal vanity," he replied imperturbably. "True, in an ideal world your opinions would be given due attention, but alas, we are forced to live in this imperfect society, where women are not only required to know their place, but to keep it."

"As I imagine your poor wife is forced to, Sir Henry," she snapped furiously. "God, how I pity her!"

"Thank you, madam," he replied icily. "I'll convey your condolences to her at the earliest opportunity."

Sophie, aware that her fury had lead her way beyond the bounds of good manners, flushed scarlet. "How like a man," she said, "to take refuge in formality to win an argument."

A flicker of real anger appeared in Hal's eyes, for this was indeed the truth. "Somebody should take a stick to you, my girl, before it is too late," he snapped, losing some of his measured calm.

"Ha! Now you offer me violence!" she cried in triumph. "Is there an iota of difference between you and Wat Rose?"

"None, save that I'd not need to be drunk to beat you!" he cried, furious that she'd roused him to anger.

"Hal," Justin laid a soothing hand on his arm, and darted him a puzzled look. "Come, let it rest. Mistress Sophia cannot but be making a May-game of us."

Hal, aware that he'd been enjoying the verbal battle

with the girl, turned aside hastily. "Aye," he replied, "so she is, and how easily the fish rose to the fly!"

Sophie eyed his averted back uncertainly, feeling suddenly that she was young and gauche, and had insulted this polished gentleman. "I, I beg pardon for my tongue, Sir Henry, it, it runs away with me at times," she said in a more gentle voice. "But, I am keeping you from your affairs. I pray you, sirs." Her glance went to Justin, but strayed back to Hal, "I pray you will not hesitate to let me know if I can be of any assistance to you!"

"By heavens, Sir Henry!" Master Benton eyed Hal with dawning respect as Sophie went quietly from the room. "You know exactly how to handle that young miss, and no mistake! I tell you, it's a great shame you are married, for you are exactly the man for her."

Hal laughed and looked shame-faced. "I have four sisters, sir, two of whom can be every bit as forceful on occasions as Mistress Sophia. I imagine years spent dealing with their tantrums has left its mark."

The older man shook his head. "This finding a husband for her is beyond me," he confessed. "When I was a lad, a lad's father arranged a marriage and that was the end of it! But these modern females are so full of themselves. I blame the war, you know, that, and allowing them to read. I should never have allowed her a tutor. My first wife never read a book in her life, yet a better woman never trod this earth. But Hannah, my sister, insisted the wench be educated. Hannah had ideas, said it was every woman's right to be able to read and write, and I gave way to her. Now look at me, left to deal with a virago!"

"Mistress Sophia is obviously a very intelligent young woman," said Justin, as Hal remained silent. "Find her an intelligent man, one she can respect as well as love, and she'll soon be tamed."

"Aye," the older man sighed heavily again, and then glanced up as they rose to go. "So, you're taking on my puzzle then, Mr Danvers?"

"I'll look into it for you, Master Benton," he replied. "More than that, I cannot promise."

❧

Chapter Four

"Poor man," remarked Justin, after they were shown out of the house and had walked down the narrow street.

Hal looked at him enquiringly.

"Well, I'd not care to be burdened with the task of safely marrying off his ward," Justin explained with a grin.

Hal, whose thoughts had been diverted by the compelling idea of taming her felt a surge of guilt and made haste to agree. "No, no indeed," he murmured, "not a task to be undertaken lightly."

Hal and Justin slowed their steps as the inn came into view and paused to discuss their next move.

"I must confess I've not seen the Common," Justin glanced towards the tollbooth, which marked the area of the market. "Perhaps it might be an idea to enquire its whereabouts of Master Blackwell."

"Or better still, Mistress Blackwell," suggested Hal.

"Aye, perhaps," grinned Justin, "especially if you don't want your head broken."

"Now, how do you know that I'd be the one to— Hello, 'tis Guy!" Hal broke off, as both he and Justin were hailed from the yard of the Greyhound.

"Justin, Hal, well met!" cried Guy Armstrong. "I was just asking the innkeeper, here, if he had any notion of your whereabouts," he threw out his hand to indicate the surly innkeeper. "Or rather, Hal's, for I wasn't expecting to see you, Justin! Mary has sent me across to invite you to Elmley Park. There can be no occasion for you to stay at an inn over the weekend, Hal, when we are so close at hand."

"But Guy, I am assisting Justin with one of his puzzles," replied Hal, his glance travelling to Adam Blackwell, who was standing looking at them with ill-concealed hostility. "I know how busy you and Mary are, what with the house to set in order, and your cousins staying."

"You can't solve a puzzle on Sunday," returned Guy, plainly primed by Mary. "Or so my dearest says, and to put it frankly, if I am not to murder my Hampshire kin before Monday, the inclusion of other, more congenial, guests is essential. In fact, if you don't want young Ned had up for murder, you'd both better come!"

"Ned?" Hal was instantly concerned. "Why?"

"Giles Durward, the eldest of the two brothers, both sons of my mother's second cousin Elizabeth, has taken a strong fancy to little Cecily. And she, for heaven alone knows what reason, appears to be encouraging his advances."

"What, sweet Cecily?" Hal was astonished. "Cecily, untrue to her Ned? I don't believe it."

"No, neither can he," replied Guy grimly. "By God, Hal, he's the image of your father when he's in a fury. He almost spits if one mentions the fellow's name, even though he's on the best of terms with the younger brother. Not that they are alike, there's six years between them. Giles is the polished, sophisticated type. He plays the lute, talks like a walking book of poetry, you know, just like that fellow Carver last year, who impressed Mary so!"

"Ambrose Carver will become your brother-in-law in due course, Guy," said Justin, who had become a great friend of Ambrose.

"Aye, if he lives that long," replied Guy, showing his excellent teeth in a grin.

"Do you tell me Cecily is besotted with this fellow, Giles Durwent, or what ever his name is?" asked Hal incredulously.

"Durward," corrected Guy, nodding gloomily. "Yes, what with him walking about the house declaiming verses, Cecily sitting in a trance gazing at him, Ned muttering under his breath and looking like a powder-keg all the time, it makes for a tricky situation."

"One you wish us to join?" asked Justin pointedly.

"Mary said I was to fetch Hal," replied Guy with the air of one disclaiming all responsibility.

"She said she knew Hal would want to talk to Ned, and if you're coming too, Justin, perhaps you could head off Giles, as you seem to have so much in common with poets."

"Nay, don't fall into a dispute over Ambrose again," said Hal at his most soothing, as Justin's eyes began to glitter, and a sharp retort rose to his tongue. "It's true, Justin, we cannot continue our questions tomorrow. At least I cannot be seen to do so, in my position, so perhaps Mary is correct. How would it be, Guy, if Justin and I rode out to Elmley Park this evening, you see, we've a few men we need to talk to first, but we could join you for supper."

"Mary will be pleased," said Guy beaming. "In fact, I'll stable my horse and give you a hand. I'm sure this puzzle work Justin undertakes isn't as difficult as it seemed last summer. What are you concerned with this time, Justin?"

"The death of one Robin Tripp, Master Benton's journeyman," Justin replied distantly.

"Tell me more about your guests," interrupted Hal hastily, knowing Justin took this work of his very seriously and that Guy considered it mere chance that Justin had found the murderer on three occasions now. "This Giles Durward, a polished sophisticate, you said? What's he doing in a country town, should he not be heading for London?"

"I don't think his pockets are too well-lined for all his talk," replied Guy. "I guess he's on the lookout for a rich wife. He speaks of coming in with me on trading ventures, but for all his talk, he has less idea of it than I, now that your father has gone, Justin." He shook his head. "I don't know, I told him straight off that Cecily was betrothed to Ned, but he doesn't seem to heed me. He says he has land in these parts, which young Jasper, his brother, confirms. But other than evicting a farmer down on his luck over Lambton way, he has hardly left our park gates."

"Perhaps he needs to escape creditors," suggested Justin. "Is he making a protracted visit?"

"Lord, I hope not!" exclaimed Guy piously. "But tell me more about this matter of the journeyman. Here, Blackwell, stable this beast for me. I'll be back for it before supper."

"Indeed, sir," the Innkeeper replied through gritted teeth. "It will be an honour."

Guy looked surprised as he turned back to join Hal and Justin. "Odd fellow, one never knows how to take him."

"With a knife in our back, I'd not be surprised," muttered Justin.

"He's not very fond of our company, Guy," explained Hal. "And he'll hate you on sight, for you've just bought his house."

"His house?" Guy repeated blankly. "What, Elmley Park? Of course, the name Blackwell! Good heavens, that's why the face is familiar! There's a fellow on one of the walls as is a dead spit of him, in an old-fashioned neck ruff."

"It would seem the Blackwells have been at Elmley Park since it was given to their ancestor by King Henry, when the Abbey's lands were taken away," said Justin knowledgeably.

"Poor fellow," said Guy with feeling. "Lost it, did he? Just like we did, paying damned Noll Cromwell's fines."

"It would seem so," agreed Hal with a sigh. "Who'd have thought it would have been better to have defied the law in the last war? So many good King's men lost everything, as I see it, for being honest men first."

"It was a very tricky decision, Hal, the Act of Indemnity," said Justin. "How do you decide on such a problem? If good money had been paid for a ruined property, then why should the new owner lose that money, whatever his political persuasion, because the King had returned? Is the King not his King too? It was a damned legal tangle I tell you, which could not be untied. The lawyers discussed it for months, and eventually it was decided the knot had to be cut. Of course, many lost, and felt it was unfair on both sides, but it was better that way."

"I lost, Hal, and your father, too," said Guy. "As luck would have it, we've made a recover, but I don't see the need to apologise for that. You accepted a rich bride, as many of us had to, to redeem your fortune. I just hit lucky on a trading venture. Bye the bye, the latest ship is weeks overdue, and I'm worried about those damn Dutch pirates. I doubt I've the bottom to be a merchant-adventurer, without your father to guide me, Justin."

Justin smiled faintly. "It will come in, never fear, I have great faith in the Navy, they'll defeat the Dutch. We are bound for the Common, Guy, I trust you know its whereabouts?"

"The Common?" he replied, pleased to show off his newly procured knowledge. "Yes, it's the other side of the river."

"Which river?" Hal asked. "The place is full of rivers."

"Aye, that's true enough. Three rivers meet here," he agreed. "Although, the Washway is but a stream until flood times. It seems it is a sight to see in the winter. The locals tell me the whole place is awash! Come, follow me, we'll take a boat."

He led the way down one of the many side alleys which formed part of the town, past a few hovels, and abruptly out onto the river. Almost at once, a boat moved into sight.

"Here, this will do," he said, clicking his fingers at

the boatman. "He'll take us across." Nimbly, he leapt into the craft and handed Justin down, whilst Hal followed. "Where do you want to go, Hal? The Common is a large place."

"To the butts," replied Hal. "And then to the Dissenters' Meeting."

"It ain't agin' the law for them to meet in the open," said the boatman defensively. "They talk a lot of blamed nonsense, but it ain't agin' the law."

"Indeed, it is not," Hal flashed the man a reassuring smile. "I merely wished to talk to one of them—a Sam Hedges, I do believe."

"Oh, Sam. Sam's a good fellow and no mistake," said the boatman satisfied. "He'll not be in any trouble, that's for sure."

"No trouble at all," Hal assured him. "My brothers and I merely wish to talk to him."

The man nodded, rowing strongly for the other side, his glance going from one to the other thoughtfully.

"There it is good and handy. The butts there, and the Meeting place." He indicated where a few people stood about, talking in small groups. "That be Sam Hedges there, that little fellow with the balding pate."

"Thank you, yes, I see him," Hal scrambled ashore

and stood helping the others. "I don't think we should advance on him in force, Justin. Why not go with Guy, and talk to those practicing with bows? See if Will Greenway is there."

Justin nodded, and strode off in company with Guy, whilst Hal strolled over to the group of men who were surveying him doubtfully. "Master Hedges?" he enquired, as he got closer.

"I'm Sam Hedges," replied the man uneasily, "do you have business with me, Sir Henry?"

Hal smiled. "I do, but nothing to do with my being a Justice," he said, aware they were uneasy, fearing their religion many be under scrutiny.

The man looked a little less harassed. "Then, I'm happy to help, sir, in any way," he agreed nervously.

"My brother-in-law, Mr Danvers and I," Hal indicated to Justin and Guy, who were conversing across the meadow with a group of men watching others fire bows and arrows, "have been asked to look into Robin Tripp's death," he said smoothly. "I understand you were one of the fire dancers, too?"

"Yes, t'was my last time," replied the man. "Since I have seen Christ risen, I've not cared for such things, but that I promised Will Greenway I'd do it, this one last time, like. We've both jumped the flames for luck these past twenty years, save at the time of Noll Cromwell, when all such things were banned as blasphemous, which indeed they are! Now my eyes have been opened, I see 'tis so. To jump the flames, is to pay homage to Satan and all his wicked works! In my youth, I was feckless and had no such thoughts. To us lads, it was a chance to show our strength. Only the strongest and bravest dare the flames."

For the few seconds, the pride was there again in his voice, then he recollected himself. "Now, of course, I see they are the fires of Hell and the temptation of the Evil One."

Hal nodded. "You have clearly reached an age of understanding and discretion," he agreed. "Who doesn't, in their youth, do things a more wiser head would condemn? But that, too, in it's way is excellent, for you'll have observed all the more clearly what was going on, on the night you jumped the fire."

"Beltane, 'tis called," he said gloomily. "I told Will we were tempting the Devil and young Robin, he overheard and laughed! Aye," he nodded, emphasising his point, "he called me old and craven, and did three cartwheels like a tumbler, before he leapt in sheer joy."

"He must have had uncommon skill," remarked Hal.

"Oh, aye!" The man was grudging in agreement. "I'm not denying he made the rest of us look like lumbering oafs! Just like quicksilver, he was," he added reminiscently. "Aye, in everything that same bright, clever quickness."

"You liked him?" asked Hal curiously.

"A fellow couldn't but help it," he admitted reluctantly. "I'd tried, since being called to God, to interest him in a return to Christ, and I have to say, he'd listen attentive enough, when he came into my shop, which is more than I could say for most. But then at the end, he'd pat my shoulder, as if to commiserate with me, he'd laugh, and cry that no doubt he was born to be hanged, and that he could never join a religion so cheerless."

Hal hid a smile. "A feckless youth indeed," he said gravely. "Tell me, Master Hedges, what exactly happened?"

"Well, it were late on," the man said, casting his thoughts back with obvious reluctance to the events of three weeks ago. "We'd all jumped once or twice, and Robin, as I say, did these cartwheels and kept dancing and throwing quips in the way he had. He'd quite a

following of sorts, and was keen to attract the notice
of Mistress Redcroft and other lasses, I dare say. Then,
when we were thinking of going again, he suddenly
jumped in front of us, and with one of his whooping
cries, leapt, and then he gave another odd cry, and fell
into the heart of the flames, it seems. I can't say for
certain, because as he took off, the wind suddenly bil-
lowed smoke our way, and before we knew it, we were
coughing and choking. Then, one of the women gave a
scream, and all the devils of Hell were let loose. People
scrabbling in the flames, and running hither and thith-
er for hooks and buckets of water," he paused, passing
a shaking hand across his pallid face. "We got him out,
dragged him free, but I could see at once it were going to be useless. He were burned black. Not a shred
of clothes left on him, and all his hair gone too!" He
finished visibly shaking, a sweat broke out on his brow
and beaded his top lip, whilst his eyes were haunted.

"A terrible end," said Hal with compassion, seeing
the graphic horror in his face.

"Aye, and a warning," said the man firmly, "if ever I
saw one. I told Will that was me finished, and he agreed
too. Well, no one who saw it, would ever want to end
up like that!"

"No," agreed Hal simply. "Tell me, for I am told it took him some time to die, too. Did it never occur to you that foul play may have been employed? Did Master Tripp say nothing, when he was pulled from the flames?"

"No," said the man, his face drawn. "He was screaming out in agony, and someone went for Master Cresswell the apothecary, but by the time he got there, the lad were shuddering and shivering, and rambling in his mind. Not that the apothecary could do much. He gave the poor fellow something for his pain, and they carried him back to Master Benton's house, where he died later."

Hal nodded his understanding. "And you saw nothing odd or unusual, either before or after the incident?"

"Odd?" said the man, puzzled. "What do you mean?"

"Something that seemed unusual, perhaps out of place," suggested Hal. "Some small thing, even, just something that wasn't as it had been the year before."

"No, it were all exactly the same," said the man dully. "The procession, the lighting of the fire, the fool, all the people gathered about…"

"Townsfolk?" interrupted Hal swiftly.

"Aye, mostly, but some out-of-town traders, too. It was a Fair that day as well, think on, aye, and some of the local gentry."

"Indeed?" said Hal. "Do you know who?"

"Nay then, I'm but a country tailor," he replied. "Gentry go to London for their clothes, they weren't none of my customers, but I did hear tell as how some of them were the new folk from Elmley Park."

Hal frowned, and opened his mouth to disagree, before thinking better of it. "Well, thank you so much for your clear and concise recollection," he said, offering the man his hand. "I know you won't accept anything for yourself, but perhaps you'll let me contribute to your charities?"

The man flushed slightly, gratified at the handshake. "That would be most welcome, Sir Henry," he said, standing a little taller. "We do have some most deserving cases amongst the poor."

"I'm sure you do," said Hal pleasantly, handing over some coins. "I know that you'll see it well-bestowed. If you should further remember anything out of the ordinary about that night, I know such memories are painful to you, but if you should, I'd be obliged if you'd come to me at the Greyhound and inform me of the circumstances."

"Right gladly, Sir Henry," said the man ducking his head awkwardly in a bow. "Right gladly."

❖

Chapter Five

Justin dropped into step beside Hal as he came to join them. "Any use?" he asked.

Hal sighed. "Not a great deal, I do believe. Yet it was odd, surely, that he thought the people from Elmley were there. Where is Guy? I must talk to him."

"He's gone to hail a boat," said Justin. "Will Greenway isn't here, the men at the butts haven't seen him in days. Somebody said something about him being sick, but another said he'd left town. So we've decided to go back to town, and enquire of his whereabouts."

Hal nodded as they came to the riverside again. "Aye, that's probably the next step. Oh, Guy, tell me, were you and Mary at this Beltane Fair, when Robin Tripp died?"

"No," said Guy, looking surprised. "I mean, we were at the fair in the afternoon, Mary wanted to see it, as it's our first year, but we left well before evening and the fire dancing. Mary said it would probably be nothing but drunken rustics.

"Ah, that must be the area of confusion," said Hal. "The tailor said some people from Elmley Park were there."

"Well, perhaps they were," said Guy thinking rapidly. "I mean, some of the servants probably went, they usually do attend fairs, and I remember Mary giving them leave. Oh, and of course, Giles and Jasper came to town in the evening, I do believe."

"So, your guests were in town the night of the Beltane fire?" Justin exclaimed. "Oh, that's excellent, Hal. We can talk to them this evening."

"Well, if you can get anything out of them," replied Guy doubtfully. "I don't understand one half of what Giles says, most of the time."

Hal followed him into the boat and scrambled into the stern. "Why?" he asked. "Is their dialect so broad?"

"No! Good Lord no," laughed Guy. "Quite the reverse. 'Tis us who are the unlettered rustics, beside the exquisite tailoring of Giles."

"Oh, I see," Hal grinned. "I foresee a very pleasant evening."

Both Hal and Justin had visited the estate Guy had purchased the previous spring, indeed, Hal had spent an uncomfortable few days there last month. Elmley Park was a lovely old house situated a few miles from Chawcester on a wooded hillside overlooking the valley. It was older than Westwood Hall, and had, since the war, suffered badly from neglect. It wasn't in the ruinous state that Hal's paternal home had been in on their return from exile, but it was obvious that it was going to take time and money to restore.

Guy had plenty of both, thanks to his ventures with Justin's father, and Mary was making inroads on the repairs. But the house was still far from finished, and visits could sometimes be a little difficult. The servants were elderly and truculent, and the odd catastrophe had been known to occur.

The latest of these appeared to be in the form of Guy's kinsfolk, two young men, offspring of a cousin of Guy's mother, whose existence Guy had heard of in his youth, but never seen. Hal wondered at his readiness in accepting them, but then recollected how good-natured he was, and how much he enjoyed his much-improved status. The temptation to show those of his extended family how well he was doing must have been too great for one who had spent the better part of his youth in penuary.

Once the introductions were made, Hal took stock of Giles and Jasper Durward. Already half-prepared by Guy's words, Hal found the conceit of the elder brother intolerable. Of a similar age to Hal, Giles had plainly established himself as a man of the world and an arbiter of good taste. On what credentials, Hal could not ascertain, unless it be pure arrogance, but it was plain that Mary, at least, had fallen under his persuasive spell. She obviously held him in great admiration, and in this she was, as ever, slavishly copied by little Cecily, Guy's sister.

Hal could easily see how it had happened. Guy and Hal's brother Ned, Cecily's betrothed, were both active hunting men. Having been in their company many a time, he knew that their day was busy and their leisure was hunting. If, at the end of that, they sat for a while with the womenfolk of their family, until they fell asleep worn out by the fresh air, their talk was of the cunning of the fox, the beauty of the stag, or the limitations of their horses. Occasionally, they might talk of the loveliness of the day or the grandness of the scenery, but only in passing.

Giles Durward was a different kettle of fish. His tailoring was so excellent, it was plain he'd never visited a country tailor. He made Hal glance at his own suit of clothes and wonder if he should not have gone to London to procure it. Was he becoming too idle, too complacent, here in the fastness of the country? Then his common sense reasserted itself. His clothes were honest clothes, well-fitted, and of good quality. What was more, they were paid for. Somehow, he doubted Giles Durward's were.

Giles's younger brother Jasper, was almost as unalike him as chalk from cheese. Hal, glancing at him, as he and Ned sat in close conversation, experienced a sense of relief so strong that he wondered at it. Here was normality, here was freshness and honesty. The lad, for he was still a stripling, was all that his elder brother was not.

Before Hal had time to consider this further, the arrival of another group of guests took his attention. He was surprised to see Master Benton accompanied by two older ladies, one of which Hal knew to be Justin's cousin, Eunice Latham, and his lovely ward Mistress Sophia.

Whilst they stood talking, and Mary began to introduce the older ladies, Hal took stock of Mistress Sophia doubtfully, wondering why she took his attention so. Obviously she was lovely, her beauty was at that stage of perfection which took the eye of everybody who beheld her. But it wasn't only that, Hal felt drawn to her, almost against his will. It was something he'd seldom felt before, a sort of magnetic attraction, a desire to be at her side, to be close to her.

Suddenly, she met his eye and smiled at him. It was a lovely smile, an overflowing of good humour, youthful spirits and anticipation of enjoyment, but it hit Hal like a bolt of lightening. It pierced the cool armour with which he surrounded himself and entered his heart.

Almost as if in response, a wave of emotion swept from his heart and colour flooded his cheeks. Abruptly, he bowed in response to her smile, to hide his feelings, and resolved to put a good distance between himself and this dangerous young woman.

In this he was lucky, as Mary sent him into dinner with Dorothy Palmer, Master Benton's widowed sister-in-law, but unfortunate in that his other neighbour was Mistress Sophia. He knew he would have to be careful.

"So, Sir Henry," Mistress Palmer said as soon as they were seated. "You are assisting Justin Danvers? Excellent, perhaps now we shall get to the bottom of this mystery."

"Mystery, ma'am?" he replied with a smile. "Yet all our efforts so far have found nothing more than a tragic accident."

"An accident, never!" she cried. "I knew Robin Tripp, let me tell you, and he wasn't the sort to put a foot wrong. That was no accident, not as I live and breathe."

"Even the best of us can make a mistake, ma'am," suggested Hal. "It would seem Robin was in high spirits, dancing and tumbling, making jests. Perhaps then, he just overplayed himself."

"My dear sir, this was not some young fool," she cried. "Robin Tripp was more than twenty years old. He'd been leaping the flames these past four years, and he leapt them properly. No cutting across the side of the fire, as many do. No, straight through the heart of it he used to go, scorching his breeches as often as not. There was none to compare with him."

"A slip then, or careless jump," suggested Hal.

She turned to look at him fully. "My dear man," she said bluntly, "why do you try so hard to make nothing of it, when it is staring you in the face?"

"Perhaps ma'am, because the whole thing lacks reason," Hal replied tartly.

"Reason," she repeated. "Oh, there is reason enough! Tell me, Sir Henry, whom do you think will inherit Edmund Benton's money, now Robin Tripp is dead?"

"The same as before. Mistress Sophia," he replied.

"Not unless she marries at the old man's will," she returned. "I can't see her doing that, can you?"

"Perhaps, ma'am, she'll find she has little choice," suggested Hal slowly.

"You look about you, Sir Henry, and see where the money will end up. Then, you'll find the reason for Robin Tripp's death, and that will give you your murderer too!" she retorted in irritation.

Hal sipped his glass of wine thoughtfully, and looked about the elegant dining room Guy had just purchased at great cost. "I'm always alive to suggestions, ma'am," he replied distantly, not caring to be drawn.

"Good heavens, would you have me do the task for you?" she cried in a sprightly manner. "Sophie is Edmund's heir, isn't that enough of a hint?"

Hal smiled his faint, aloof smile. "You have our friend the surly innkeeper in mind? I own, I could easily favour him as a villain, from the fact that he never fails to let me know how much he dislikes me. But a court of law, you know, would require rather more. Proof of intent, firstly, and a court of law wouldn't even consider what I believe is called feminine intuition."

"Pooh!" she cried robustly. "How like a man to dismiss a thing that will require some effort, as a mere figment of feminine intuition. Do you imagine Blackwell to be the only suitor of one so lovely?"

"I stand corrected," he replied bleakly. Of course, somebody as desirable as Mistress Sophia must have many suitors. He knew that and accepted it as normal, but couldn't help feeling suddenly very low in spirits. "I mentioned Blackwell as the most likely suitor, but I shall be happy to be informed of any others."

"Look about you," she commanded, waving her hand to indicate the table at large. "And multiply that twenty fold! Sophie has beauty, money and enough breeding to be a prize to almost any man. Ask about the table which man, save perhaps our host, who is plainly besotted, wouldn't like to have such a wife as this?"

Hal, who'd been thinking that if Mistress Palmer in any way resembled Master Benton's sister Hannah, then he knew the author of the heiress's obstinacy, sat back and observed the table. The attention Cecily Armstrong was receiving from the exquisite Giles Durward was something to behold. Hal had to admit to a strong fellow-feeling of indignation, as charm was lavished upon his brother's betrothed, whilst Ned himself sat by in a tongue-tied fury.

Meanwhile, Sophie had been examining her fellow guests at the table. So, these were the members of the Armstrong-Westwood connection. Guy himself sat at the head, he was a very pleasant-looking man with dark hair, a small pointed beard, and a quick impatient manner. His sister, Cecily, sat not far from Guy, next to Justin Danvers, who was a rather bookish and undistinguished-looking companion of Sir Henry Westwood. Cecily, on the other hand, was a pretty, fair-haired girl, dressed in a gown of blue brocade, caught up over a cream satin petticoat. Sophie knew that she was betrothed to Ned Westwood, and envied her her London dressmaker, for both she and Mary, Guy's wife, were dressed in the height of fashion. Although, Sophie knew Master Benton would never allow her to wear a gown with so tight-laced and low-cut a bodice as Mary wore, even if the expensive lace did give it an impression of modesty. Mary's beauty had become something of a legend in the small town of Chawcester, and certainly, beside the provincial clothes of Mistress Latham, and the dowdy gown of Mistress Palmer, the newcomers looked to be all that was bright, fashionable and fascinating to Sophie, not the least being Sir Henry Westwood. Sophie allowed her gaze to flicker over him as he sat talking to Mistress Palmer. His dark hair was fashionably curled and hung down to beneath his shoulders. He wore a blue coat of the French fashion with a long waistcoat and wide turned-back cuffs. At his throat, he wore a cravat, which tied in a bow under his masterful jawline.

"One cannot but agree with your earlier comment Mistress Palmer," Hal said, nodding after a few moments. "Although, of course, many of us about the table are married. But, those who are not, appear to be trying to fix their interest."

"What, that little charade?" the older woman replied with a scornful laugh. "Oh, don't be taken in by that, Sir Henry! That's merely Mr Durward, strutting like the peacock he is! He's flaunting his feathers to show Sophie how wonderful Cecily thinks he is! If that pretty little thing wasn't such an innocent, and your young brother wasn't showing quite such a resemblance to a thundercloud, that little flirtation would have died out days ago."

Hal's lips thinned with displeasure. "I have no patience with the type of man who would cause such distress to minister to his own vanity."

"Indeed, the fellow's a fool and a cockscomb," she replied tartly. "But he'll never marry to disoblige himself, he holds himself too high. Cecily Armstrong's dowry couldn't meet with his pretensions. To his mind, wealth must be met with a wealthy wife."

Hal nodded his understanding of the situation, and as her attention was claimed by Justin, Hal took the opportunity to engage Mistress Sophia's attention, telling himself it was necessary for the enquiry. "So, Mistress Redcroft, we meet again," he said. "I did not expect the pleasure quite so soon."

Sophie glanced to him, wondering if his tone was one of irony. After he'd left that afternoon, she'd convinced herself, in a storm of tears, that she'd behaved very ill and given him a great dislike of her. Then, came Mistress Latham's message, and she'd set about securing their attendance, in the face of Master Benton's reluctance. "Mistress Latham wished for Uncle Edmund's escort," she said quickly. "And I have long wished to meet Mistress Armstrong, for I'd heard how lovely she is." She looked up at him shyly, comparing the elegant poise of their heads, the similar cast of nose and the thick, dark silky hair.

"She is your sister, is she not?"

"Mary, yes, she is my sister," he agreed. His gaze followed hers to where Mary sat at the foot of the table, listening with every evidence of sympathy, to Master Benton's discourse. Her lovely head was inclined politely, her sweet face registering nothing but rapt attention to his words. "And yes, she was considered something of a beauty in her youth."

"Oh sir, she still is," Sophia cried. "Mistress Armstrong is still yet young."

"I'm relieved to hear you say so," he replied, smiling. "She is my elder by a clear thirteen months."

"That I was not aware of, although I saw the likeness at once," she replied artlessly. "Although I must confess, Mr Edward Westwood confuses me, for he looks nothing like either of you."

"No, Ned is like my father, my late father," he replied, the smile dying on his lips. "Mary and I share a mother, who died giving birth to me. Ned and my younger sisters, are the offspring of my father's subsequent marriage." He met Ned's angry eyes and forced an encouraging smile. "Neither is Ned usually so very grim looking," he added as his young face relaxed a little. "I rather fear he is far from happy at the attention Durward is heaping upon his betrothed."

"No," agreed Sophie, her eyes going to Cecily's flushed face. "I can imagine he is not best pleased."

"Or you either, Mistress Redcroft?" he asked bluntly. "For have I not heard a rumour that Mr Durward seeks your favour?"

"Dame Rumour, sir, is a fool, a strumpet, puffed up by lies and half-truths," she replied evasively. For some inexplicable reason, she was unable to bear Hal thinking she might even tolerate Giles Durward.

Hal smiled a little, seeing her ploy. "I see you are a gentlewoman of great sense, ma'am, and will keep your own counsel."

"I'll certainly not be apportioned in marriage without my consent, sir," she replied firmly. "When I marry —and I am in no great hurry to do so—it will be because I love and respect the man I have chosen."

"Bravo! I applaud your strong mind," he said politely. "Respect is indeed essential in marriage; love, affection that can come later."

"As in your case, sir?" she asked quickly.

Hal looked taken aback at her question. "Well, certainly I had not previously met the lady who was to be my wife before our wedding," he agreed.

Sophie had the feeling he'd withdrawn behind a veneer of ice. "But surely, sir, it is so very easy, as in little Cecily Armstrong's case, to get caught too young, before one knows one's own mind?" she asked earnestly.

Hal looked startled. "Cecily and Ned are devoted," he replied sharply. "Cecily is more than content with her choice."

"If she was that happy, she'd not be entertaining Giles Durward's attentions at all," replied Sophie astutely, "but send him about his business in no uncertain terms."

"You do not make allowances for a more pliable temper," Hal said quickly. "I doubt Cecily would know how."

Sophie smiled at him saucily. "Excuse me, Sir Henry, but don't you think perhaps your brother could be a little dull?"

"Ned?" he cried indignantly. "No, never, not dull! But," he sighed faintly, "perhaps not the best fellow in the world at courting a maid."

"Exactly," she replied. "From my observations, his conversation consists mostly of the excellent runs he's had at the chase, and how dear his companion dogs are to him. It is my maxim, that if a man is dull before marriage, he'll be ten times duller after."

"Dear me," said Hal coolly. "Perhaps I begin to see why you are wary of marriage."

She chuckled, but reddened and looked a little disconcerted, saying daringly: "Come Sir Henry, don't look down your handsome nose at me, you know 'tis so, and that I am right to be cautious."

"Is Giles Durward such excellent company then?" he asked, unable to prevent a smile for she had very winning ways, and there was no offence in her words, only fun.

"Not to compare with yours," she replied, her head spinning a little from the warmth of his smile. "Understand, Giles is only too aware of how charming he is, and that he is greatly honouring one by the bestowal of such attentions as he chooses to dispense."

Hal laughed abruptly. "Mistress Sophia, you have no chance of making a marriage at all, with thoughts like that in your head," he said wryly.

She smiled too, feeling absurdly elated to have made him laugh. "I rather think, Sir Henry, I've been spoiled for marriage anyway," she replied quickly, "for I've a horrid feeling I've met the very man for me, and discovered he's already taken."

Hal smiled again, puzzled by this. "My condolences in that case, ma'am. But, I think you are rather young to take such a decision. I do agree with you in one thing. If you have any doubts, delay your decision, and what is more, I'll see Cecily gets the chance to delays hers."

"I thought I understood from Mistress Palmer's conversation that your brother had fixed his wedding for next January," Sophia replied, surprised at his words.

"Indeed," he agreed, "but if Cecily has some doubts, it would be better that she delays it further, until she is sure in her own mind."

"Will your brother countenance that, sir?" she asked doubtfully.

"He will be very unhappy," he agreed. "But better that he be unhappy for a short while, than they both enter a marriage of misery."

She nodded, well satisfied by his answers, and before she could speak, the conversation became more general, with Giles asking insolently in a loud voice: "Who is your wine merchant, cousin? I mean to lay in a stock at my farmhouse, which I shall use as a hunting lodge from time to time, but if this is the best Chawcester can offer, I needs must go further afield!"

Guy looked uncomfortable. "We are indebted to Master Benton for this evening's wine," he said, hoping to turn it into a jest. "I must confess, it rather suits my palate." He glanced desperately to Hal for assistance.

"Indeed, thought it a good burgun..." began Hal, but Durward cut in rudely.

"This wine wasn't purchased to suit any's palate, more their pocket."

"My good friend Alderman Chegleigh left me that wine in his will," said Master Benton wrathfully. "A full pipe of it he had in his cellar, back in '58."

"It has not travelled well," said Durward loftily.

"I brought it here in the saddlebags," said the Malt-ster defensively.

"A good wine should travel by water only," sneered Durward.

"Well, it would be hard-pressed to get up this hill, even if it had been floated down the river from Chaw-cester," said Guy laughing uneasily. "And I daresay it makes little odds, anyway. It tastes excellent to me, Master Benton. Your very good health."

Hal promptly joined him in the toast, forcing the table to follow, even Giles Durward in a surly manner. But Edmund Benton's face had taken on a ghastly hue, and he clasped his hand across his jutting stomach.

"Are you in pain again, Uncle Edmund?" asked Sophie in concern.

"But a little," he replied, fumbling at his pouch. He glanced in apology to Mary, adding: "I beg you'll excuse me Mistress Armstrong, that fancy French quack in town says I mustn't get upset whilst I am eating, and has given me these things to chew." He smiled wryly. "The trouble is, it's often difficult not to get upset, when confronted by idle good-for-nothings who imagine they know everything."

"Indeed," Mary said, hastily fixing her kinsman with a look.

"I was merely going to suggest, Mary, that Master Benton tries some wine I always carry with me. It may be a little dry to his taste, but I can vouch for its excellence."

"Thank ye, thank ye, but I'll not trouble," said the Maltster truculently. "I'm in no mood now to appreciate any wine."

"I am given to understand, Mr Durward, that you and your brother were present in the crowd that watched the fire dancers back in May," said Justin hastily, hoping to give the conversation a fresh turn.

"Indeed," agreed Giles, inclining his head so that his heavy, full wig fell forward. "We were in attendance on Mistress Redcroft."

"That was earlier on," said Sophie sharply, still not willing for Hal to know that she liked or encouraged Giles' attentions, "before the fire dancing. You weren't with us during the dancing."

Durward smiled slightly. "I was never far from your side, Mistress Sophia. Jasper and I were a little behind you, I do believe, for Master Benton pushed forward to see his man leap the flames." His obsequious expression sobered. "Such a tragic occurrence, it quite discomposed one. Yet one can't quite help feeling that it was such a fruitless errand at any event. With all due respect to the poor, dead, young man, what was the use of it all?"

"A following of tradition, one must suppose," replied Hal, as Master Benton subjected the objectionable young man to a hard stare. "The 'why' doesn't concern us, merely the outcome, and whether there was some suggestion of foul play."

"Foul play?" said Jasper Durward, who spoke in surprise. "How so? Surely the poor fellow tripped? Not that it was easy to see, because of the sudden smoke, but that's what I assumed."

"Another mentioned smoke," observed Hal. "What happened? Did the wind get up?"

"Not that I remember," said the young man thoughtfully. "We'd walked to another part of the fire, and then you said something about needing to relieve yourself, Giles," he added innocently, as his elegant brother glared at him. "So I continued walking, then, as I say, this billowing smoke filled the air. It made people cough and masked off all the dancing for a while. Then, there was a terrible scream, and people began running. I ran with them, and helped two fellows drag what I thought was, at first, a bundle of clothes, from the fire." He shuddered. "Poor fellow, he was in agony!" He looked up to meet Sophie's eyes, "I'm sorry Mistress Sophia, I'm a clumsy fool to talk about it."

"No," she said from white lips. "If Robin was killed, we need to talk about it. I was very fond of him. I would never have married him, but I was fond of him, and I feel no more pain than any that knew him."

"How could he have been killed?" asked Giles scornfully. "The fool must have tripped in the smoke."

"Robin could have done that leap with his eyes shut," growled Master Benton. "The smoke wouldn't have troubled him."

"What are you suggesting, then?" asked Jasper. "That he was tripped? Or pushed?"

"He couldn't have been tripped," said Sophie. "He was like a tumbler, he'd have righted himself. But a push, yes, that's possible."

"No, it's impossible!" cried Giles. "Why a man would have to be almost in the flames himself, to push him." He glanced uncertainly about the table, "Would he not?"

"Well, yes, one would suppose so," agreed Justin. "And perhaps that is a line of thought. Many were present, but surely only the fire leapers should have been scorched or smoky."

"No, by the time it was over, we were all smoky," said Jasper. "My doublet still stinks of smoke, in spite of being aired this past week. Aye, and the sleeve is scorched, for the heat trying to get him out was intense."

"Where there many about you at this time?" asked Hal.

"Oh, it was complete confusion," he replied. "People calling, poor Robin crying out at first. Other people running, falling over each other in the smoke, a crowd gathering." Again, he shuddered. "It was dreadful!" he repeated quietly. He glanced up again, gave a small smile and shook himself like a dog ridding himself of water. "Forgive me, but it still makes me uneasy. I can't explain the horror of it. Lit by the lurid light of the flames one moment, coughing on the smoke the next, complete confusion."

"Aye, t'was so," agreed Master Benton heavily. "Confusion, t'was worse than a battlefield. Poor lad, poor lad."

Guy glanced to Mary in dismay, to see tears in her eyes. "Poor young man, indeed," he said quickly. "And plainly held in great affection! All the more reason to delve into this fully, eh, Justin? To see justice done?"

"Oh, aye," replied Justin quietly. "We'll see justice done if at all possible, won't we, Hal?"

"Indeed." Hal agreed solemnly. "We'll get to the bottom of this affair, one way or another."

❧

Chapter Six

It was the next morning when Giles Durward glanced about the deserted hall, all his companions had long since set off for church as was expected, save for the ageing merchant. Notwithstanding his rudeness the previous evening, it was Durward's intention to ask for Sophie in marriage, and he had no doubt he could overcome the other's antagonism if put to it. An evening spent in Sophie's company had finally convinced Durward that she was the woman for him. The half-formed plan of cutting Ned Westwood out had been abandoned on the twin peaks of little Cecily's meekness of character, which would make her an easily-intimidated wife, and her more modest dowry. His needs were pressing, and whilst the glittering prize of Sophie was within reach, he must try for it. He came upon Master Benton finishing a late breakfast in a sunny parlour. "Ah! Good morning, sir," he said, entering the comfortable room.

"I trust I see you returned to your excellent good health this morning."

"Oh, 'tis you, Durward," replied the merchant, glaring at him. "Yes, I thank you."

"And that you'll allow me to apologise wholeheartedly, for my inadvertent rudeness last evening. I must confess if I'd known the wine was of your providing, I would never have said a word. My dear cousin Guy, though an excellent fellow, has little idea of these things. As a connoisseur of the grape, I sought to guide him, in my clumsy way, to perhaps spending a little more on his cellar."

Master Benton eyed him doubtfully. He disliked the man intensely, but feared him too. He knew he was aiming high in coming here to a gentleman's house to try to ally his Sophie, and but that the Westwoods had already entered into marriage with a differing class, he'd have never dared. To find an exquisite of this calibre had quite unnerved him, and given him pause for thought. If the Westwoods were out of the question, and both Sophie's reply and that of Sir Henry had been equivocal, then why not one of their kinsmen?

"Your apology is accepted," he said stiffly, not sure how to express himself.

"Ah, you are goodness itself," Giles Durward sat down and poured himself a mug of ale. "I am so pleased to get that out of the way, because I did want to have some discussion with you about your ward."

"Sophie?" he rasped. "What about her?"

"Well now, I understand you are anxious to see her well-matched," he said.

"Not anxious," the Maltster corrected him. "I have no worries that I shall indeed do so."

"No, none? Not even Blackwell?" returned Giles innocently.

"Blackwell is nothing." The merchant was dismissive.

"I am relieved to hear you say so," Giles kept his temper with an effort. "May one then be permitted to put forward a suggestion?"

"You may," he agreed, "but I give no promises."

"Naturally," said Giles. "But I would like to suggest myself as a future husband for your ward."

"And why should I look upon you with favour," he asked coldly, "when I've watched you flirt with that child Cecily all weekend?"

"Pooh! A mere bagatelle," he cried laughing. "A sweet child to amuse one on a rainy day. If I'd thought my cousinly kindness was to be misunderstood, I'd have kept my distance."

"You've a very ready tongue, young man," said the merchant shrewdly. "But I noticed you don't say just why I should favour you above any other."

Giles affected mock dismay. "And I, in my conceit, thought my person spoke for me," he replied cunningly. "But if you would have me list my attributes: item one—gentleman of landed estate; item two—quick intelligence; item—"

"Landed estate—" interrupted the merchant. "How many acres?"

"Oh, good heavens, I am no clerk to keep figures in my head. Four or five hundred," he replied airily.

"Unencumbered?" demanded the Maltster.

"Aye, there's the rub," laughed the gentleman. "Not all, unfortunately! We suffered reverses in the war years you know, and thereafter. Wheat prices hit lows, but you are a man of the world, you know all this. And that it takes but a little money, a wealthy bride, to set many of us back on the road to fortune again, much like Sir Henry Westwood. Where would he be without a judicious marriage?"

Edmund Benton listened with but half an ear as the words slipped out easily. It might be so, it might not he'd find that all out by and by. In the meantime, there was Sophie to be thought of. "And if I were to give my consent—and mind, I say, if—" said the merchant, "do you think Sophie would agree?"

"My dear sir, my very dear sir, I can handle females," Durward replied laughing. "Your sweet Sophie? I could, if I had a mind to it, have her eating out of my hand by dinnertime."

Edmund Benton laughed. The chuckle began in his chest, and rose into his throat, at the monstrous conceit of the fellow. "Well, my fine lad, you are welcome to try," he gasped. "By heavens, she'll make mincemeat of you!"

"Sir, you mistake." Durward's eyes had grown hard at the other's amusement, and a deadly anger bit at him. None, but none, laughed at Giles Durward.

"I think the boot's on the other foot, my lad," Master Benton chuckled. "I think the boot's on the other foot!"

Durward sat icily until the other's laughter had ceased, then he said, with some emphasis: "Do I take it I have your permission to address myself to your ward?"

"Aye, you may try your luck, but then, I think you've been doing that all your life, haven't you?" The merchant nodded his head sagely. "Mayhap you're what I need for Sophie, if what you say is true. Mayhap you're not, I give you no encouragement."

"But I take it, from even being allowed to try," Durward replied, back to his most urbane. "And if I fail, mayhap we can still toast each other in that wine I spoke of?"

Edmund Benton shook his head, "I doubt me my insides are up to it," he sighed.

"I assure you, sir, this wine will sit like ambrosia in your stomach," Durward replied, draining his tankard and getting to his feet. "In the meantime, I'm away to try my fortune with Mistress Sophia."

Hal sat in the pew, his head resting in his clenched fists, which in turn rested on the pew in front, his eyes shut tight.

He'd sat thus ever since the service ended, seeming at prayer, but in fact waiting, waiting for the church to clear, so that he should be alone to stem the chaos of his thoughts and emotions. Never before in his life had he felt so at the mercy of events. He'd accompanied his sister Mary and her husband to church this morning, like any well-bred guest, and slipped into the pew with no thoughts other than those which had occupied him overnight. Then, she had sat down beside him, handed into the pew by Justin, and the well-ordered calm of his life had been shattered.

He loved Libby, he adored little Harry and the baby Francis. These were the bedrock of his existence, and he must cling to them. Libby had been a good and faithful wife to him for more than five years, and the bonds of affection were firm, even when he'd been led astray by feelings of lust for his father's wife, Jacqueline. So, why now should this young woman affect him in such an overwhelming manner? There were no other words for it. He'd been aware of her with every fibre of his body, with each atom of his existence. Their hands had touched as she'd reached for her hymnal, and a burning fire had swept through him, bewildering his thoughts, even as it weakened his resistance. It filled him with a wild desire to crush her into his arms. Even now, as he sat shaken and confused, his nostrils were still filled with the soft scent of her, and his skin still craved the brush of her arm as she rose to leave, the cobweb kiss of the edge of her silken gown.

He sat up, forcing his brain from its kaleidoscope of fragmented pictures, opening his eyes on the bright patches of coloured light from the stained glass window, so recently dug up from its hiding place in the churchyard and restored to its glory by the Rector.

At least nobody knew his complete disarray, that must be his only consolation. None could see his heart, thank God, and he must keep his feelings checked and his emotions concealed under a cloak of polished manners. It was only for the duration of the day. This evening, he and Justin would be back in Chawcester, and they never need be in Sophia Redcroft's company again.

The feeling of despair, which swept over him at this thought, dismayed him. Was this what it was like to truly be in love? Had he indeed been smug and self-satisfied previously? Prepared to condemn his fellow man for extravagant folly, when he'd no experience of the malady?

Decisively, he got to his feet, many were crossed in love. He'd be no different to countless others. His way was clear, he was a married man, a respected member of his community, he had no choice but to crush his emotions. It was now a good ten minutes since the rest of his party had departed, and he could hear the verger shuffling his feet impatiently, his thoughts probably on his dinner, fast going cold.

Awarding the man a coin for his trouble, he stepped out into the cool of a pearly grey morning. The early sun was hidden behind a pall of grey cloud, and there was the faintest tendency to missle. Hal put his hat firmly on his head and strode up the path, stopping short in dismay at the lych-gate.

"Oh, Mr Westwood," Sophie smiled blindingly at him. "Mr Durward and I were talking, and have quite been left behind."

Something in her manner conveyed to him her dislike of her companion, and her relief at his arrival, which would enable her to escape. But he ignored the appeal, knowing his own resolve to be too fragile. "Then pray, don't let me interrupt you," he said swiftly, with a smile. "Far be it for an old married man like myself to halt another's progress."

"Nay sir," she put out a hand, detaining his arm, her fingers biting into his flesh through his coat and shirt-sleeve, desperate in their demand. "You interrupt nothing! Mr Durward and I have nothing further to say to each other, and I would beg the escort of a married man back to Mr Armstrong's house."

Such an appeal could not be denied. Hal resigned himself to another fifteen minutes of purgatory, feeling them only justly applied, for allowing himself such thoughts as he'd been indulging in previously. "Then pray, allow me the pleasure of such an escort," he replied smoothly, with a bow. "Mistress Redcroft, your servant." He offered her the arm she still clutched. "Mr Durward, yours."

With Hal's hat swept low and firmly replaced, Giles Durward had no choice but to retire from his position, barring the exit from the lych-gate. He, too, bowed, but with ill grace, muttering under his breath.

"What have you done to anger that poppin-jay, my pretty?" Hal found himself saying, to his own fury, for he'd resolved as he'd taken her arm, to keep on strictly formal terms, as they walked swiftly away.

"Refusing his offer of marriage," she replied, in a suffocated voice. "As civilly as I could at first, but with mounting dismay and anger, as he refused to accept it."

His heart leapt in a like anger at the thought of the other's impudence, but he said coolly, "Well, no harm done, then. After all, you can't blame him for pressing his case. You are a darling."

She glanced up at him, surprised into laughing. He met her eyes and was lost. "But I do blame him, sir," she said, tears filling her eyes. "And I do not appreciate his methods of persuasion! When I want to be kissed, I'll volunteer my hands and my lips."

Hal licked his own, and with a tremendous effort looked away. "Quite right, too," he agreed, his voice shaking with suppressed desire. "They are yours to withhold at will."

"Thank you, sir," she said with tears sounding in her voice. "I knew I could rely upon you to rescue me."

"You are welcome, ma'am." He replied formally, then as she gave a little sob, he glanced back, looked into her blue-violet eyes drowned in tears, and knew that he was drowning too. "Oh Sophie, Sophie, don't," he whispered.

"Why not?" she asked, not bothering to dissemble.

"Because I am a married man," he replied, "I cannot love you."

"Do you have a choice?" she asked softly. "I don't. You smiled at me yesterday, and that was it. Since then, everything has been different."

"No, no, no," he cried. "This is mere infatuation! A spring madness that will depart as soon as it arrived! Don't refine too much upon it. I am a married man. You must make a good marriage. It is nothing, I tell you! Nothing!"

"So do you love your wife?" she asked, ignoring this.

"Indeed I do," he replied quickly. "Libby is my good friend, the mother of my children. I love and respect her."

"As much as you love me?" she asked, tears sliding down her cheeks, in the face of so sure and comprehensive an answer.

"Much, much more," he lied, his heart crying out in pain to see her so distressed. "A thousand times more. Oh, Sophie, I pray you, don't do this. There is no future for us, my darling, I cannot, I will not love you. I have other responsibilities! Please don't make this so hard for us both."

"But I love you," she whispered brokenly. "My heart has never felt like this before. I have never wanted to kiss a man until I saw your face. Now I want to kiss every inch of it. I want to feel your arms about me, your lips on mine, your hands caressing me. To hear you tell me—"

"Don't!" he cried in real anguish. "Don't! Don't, Sophie! That way lies madness!"

As the trees of the lane closed about them, she swung round to face him. "Kiss me!" she commanded. "If you are going to leave me today without a backward glance,

I must have something to live on! Kiss me and convince me that this is nothing but spring madness."

He stared into her passionate face as if in a daze, his hands unconsciously tightened his grip on her upper arms. For a few seconds. he toyed with the idea of shaking her, and stalking off in high dugeon, but the temptation was irresistible. He bent his head and succumbed to the lure of her soft plump lips.

Reeling like a drunkard, he pulled away, his head spinning, his legs suddenly like jelly. He raised an unsteady hand to his mouth as if to capture the kiss, and stood so for a few moments.

"Why do you turn from me?" she whispered, leaning her golden head against his broad back. "Do you think after that you can lie to me again?"

"Come, we must go back," he said, and his voice rang starkly.

"What, no other kiss?" she whispered, bringing her hands to rest either side of her head on the cloth of his coat, as she gently kissed it. "Are you finished with me so swiftly?"

"Mistress Redcroft, this is no conduct befitting a gentlewoman," he replied austerely. "I beg you will take my arm and I'll escort you to my sister's house, where we must—and shall part—for the sanity of us both."

"Do not think you can forget me, for I'll not let you," she replied, not heeding him, but continuing to kiss the cloth of his coat, so that he was aware of it across his broad back.

He broke free and began to quickly walk away. "If you will not walk with me, I shall have to leave you," he said in reply, his voice shaking.

She hurried to catch him, slipping her hand through his arm. "You shall not escape me so lightly," she said hugging the arm and rubbing her face against his sleeve in a manner he found devastating.

"I shall always be with you now! When you close your eyes, you'll see my face. As you lay down to sleep, you'll feel me in your arms. Every time your lips meet, you'll remember my kiss."

"Stop!" he groaned. "Be still! This will not do!"

"Tonight as you put your head to your pillow, think of me, no more than a hundred yards from your door. Think of me stretched out in that great bed—"

He put his hands to his ears. "Be silent!" he harshly commanded. "You shall not torment me."

She laughed shakily under her breath. "Torment you?" she repeated. "Where do I torment you? I call to you, my soul reaches out to yours. We are as one, Hal, nothing, not time, nor place, nor people, can stop that! We are as one, and you shall not withstand it."

"I must!" he cried, almost running in his haste to be rid of her.

She laughed again and suited her stride to his. "You cannot escape fate, Hal. Fate dogs your steps and calls to you. You can run from it, but not hide."

"Mistress Redcroft," he said, making a tremendous effort. "You are little better than a child, so hold your tongue as I bid you! We are in sight of my sister's house. I demand you behave with propriety."

"And I demand you heed my call, Hal," she countered. "Come to me, or I shall seek you."

Hal sighted Justin, standing in the doorway of the old house, a puzzled frown on his face. "Oh, thank God," he muttered and strode on. "Justin," he called, as soon as he was in hailing distance, "Is ought amiss?"

"No," Justin replied slowly, seeing his companion.

"Mistress Redcroft met with some trouble in the form of an importuning lover," Hal explained hurriedly. "We left Mr Durward to his own devices. As, ma'am, I shall now leave you, having safely delivered you to the door."

"Thank you, Hal," she replied meekly. "I am grateful for your interference. There is nothing so despicable, to my mind, than a man who'll make love to a maid and then abandon her."

"Nothing," he agreed, unable to meet her eyes. "But you must take greater care, Mistress Redcroft, that you are not in the company of such villains without a chaperone."

"Odd young woman," remarked Justin, as she departed with a glowing look for Hal.

"She is little more than a child," said Hal uneasily.

"Some of the looks she casts you are far from childlike," replied Justin shrewdly, aware Hal was evading him in some way. "Did you say you rescued her from Giles Durward?"

"Yes, it seems he'd been offering his heart, and didn't like her refusal." Hal bent to straighten a wrinkle in his stocking, so as not to have to meet Justin's eyes.

Justin tutted. "The fool should have addressed her uncle anyway," he said. "And I suppose now he'll not speak to you."

"I shouldn't be surprised," agreed Hal. "Not that he was particularly forthcoming anyway."

"True," agreed Justin, gloomily. "In fact, I don't think

we have made any progress at all, do you?"

"No," said Hal, after a few moments thought. "As I see it, there is a likelihood Robin Tripp was murdered, but we are never going to be able to prove it."

Justin sighed, "Yes, I think you are right, but I'll give it just a little longer. Will you go and find Jasper Durward, and see if he can shed any more light on the evening of the fire, and I'll try his elder brother again. Then, tomorrow, whilst you are in court, I'll seek out Wat Rose and Will Greenway, and if there is still nothing, I'll report to Master Benton, and leave it at that."

Hal nodded his agreement and soon departed on his errand.

Meanwhile, Giles Durward, balked of his main prey, and with a score to settle with regard to the Westwoods, came upon Cecily, gathering flowers in the badly neglected garden. "Good afternoon Mistress Cecily," he said at once. "Are you well? I missed your sweet presence this morn."

"No, I have the headache," she replied. "Mary told me to walk in the garden in the fresh air rather than sit in the stuffy church. I shall, of course, go to evensong."

"But of course," he replied. "None could doubt your sweet piety, any more than your sweet face. May I walk with you?"

Confusion spread over Cecily's face. She'd been hoping Ned might seek out her company, for surely, he too must have missed her in church. She didn't like her new kinsfolk, for Giles frightened her, and Jasper spent every available minute with Ned. "Well, I am not entirely certain…" she began, for only yesterday, Ned had come upon them sitting on a sheltered seat in the garden, and kicked up a dreadful fuss which had led to an awful quarrel. Yet how could she make it up with Ned, if Giles was at her side again?

"Don't worry," he said, his smile wry and slightly amused, so that she felt, as she always did when he spoke, young, foolish and inexperienced. "If we should sight your jealous, rustic lover, I shall instantly leap over that wall, and hide myself with the pigs."

His words made her laugh uneasily, for everything was said in a half-jesting manner, that put her at a great disadvantage, and made it very difficult for her to dispute. And so, without any consent on her part, they continued their walk.

"Whither are you bound?" he asked politely.

"Oh, I thought I'd walk to the lake," she replied evasively, knowing that they'd be in full view of the windows there, so she couldn't be unjustly accused, as on the previous day, of sneaking in corners with him. "I saw some beautiful iris and some bull rushes there, which will look pretty, I think."

He glanced to the flowers in her hand. "You gather for effect then, not for health. You are not gathering for a brew to help the headache."

"No," she replied. "Libby makes our simples, she is a very good herbalist, but I don't know enough, and brews invariably make me sick."

"Ah, I am of your opinion. Don't they always taste horrid?" he asked, making a comical face. "But my mother, like Lady Westwood, grew all manner of herbs, and frequently took Jasper and I on foraging expeditions, to help her bring home her spoils! I, therefore, know most herbs. See, this mallow is quite striking, shall I gather some?"

"Is it mallow, oh yes, that's pretty. Please do," she replied quickly.

"And here, at the foot of the wall, parsley, that will make a pretty addition, will it not, to your bunch?"

"Oh no, oh it smells disagreeable," cried Cecily, pulling away as he offered her several plucked sprigs.

"Oh, so it does," he agreed, sniffing it and making another comical face. "I'll throw it away then. But stay, no, instead I'll gather more, for I do believe this is a sovereign remedy, so my groom tells me, for horses, and my poor mount is so afflicted at the moment, I am forced to borrow a horse from Guy."

"Ned is very good with horses," sighed Cecily.

"He had to be good at something, of course," he agreed.

"He is very good at lots of things," cried Cecily stung. "None hunts as well as he, no, nor is a better rider—"

"Well, you'll never go hungry then, if he can fill the pot with game, when you are wed," smiled Giles silkily. "It must be comforting to think you'll never have an empty stomach. Of course, you might well be driven to distraction by boredom…"

"Ned is very interesting," she cried indignantly. "You just don't understand. You don't see his good, clever side."

"If you tell me there is one, Mistress Cecily, I have no doubts," he said smoothly. "Now, that patch of ladies' smock, shall you have some of those for your bouquet?"

❧

Whilst Giles was gently wooing Cecily, Hal finally found Jasper in the company of Ned, both engaged in throwing horseshoes in a desultory manner.

"Well, what else is there to do on a Sunday afternoon in the country?" asked Ned, as Hal frowned.

"I wish to heaven I'd stayed at home, rather than come here to be made a May-game of."

"He's quarrelled with the fair Cecily," explained Jasper, hitting the post with unnerving skill.

"Quarrelled with sweet Cecily, I'd not have thought it possible," exclaimed Hal, taken aback, for Cecily's pliable temper was a byword.

"Not easy, but not impossible," replied Jasper. "Ned decided to become heavy-handed and objected to Cecily sitting talking to Giles yesterday evening."

"Not talking," cried Ned wrathfully. "They were hid away in the garden, cuddling and kissing!" His throws missed the stake completely.

"Cecily?" cried Hal. "I cannot believe it of her, she is a very modest maid."

"Giles has quite a way with him you know," said Jasper, scoring another hit.

"I told her I'd not tolerate such behaviour from my

betrothed," interrupted Ned. "And that in future, she'd better not speak to any man, and she said to me, and she said—" He opened his mouth and shut it several times, as if he were still unable to credit what his beloved had said. "She said, that was a matter soon remedied. Our betrothal could be at an end, and that if I thought I had any right to lecture her, I was very much mistaken."

In spite of his sympathy for his brother's plight, Hal had to master the desire to smile. Ned was so patently out of his depth. "Dear me," he said hastily. "She does seem put out by something, doesn't she? Did you ask her what had irked her?"

"I did," cried Ned, abandoning his game in his haste to explain, as Jasper made a third hit. "I said for her not to get in such a silly pucker, and to tell me what was amiss, so I could arrange everything! And do you know what she replied?" he cried, banging his fist into his other hand in exasperation. "She said if I didn't know what was wrong, she wasn't going to tell me! There! How is a fellow supposed to deal with that sort of reply?"

"Tricky," agreed Hal, trying desperately not to laugh. "I imagine you'll just have to think and think, until you come up with the answer."

"Well, I have then," scowled Ned. "Jasper and I've

been talking and talking, and we can't see what I've done wrong. It's not as if I've hunted everyday or anything. I don't go above two or three times a week now, as she doesn't like it. No, I've been here most days, practicing archery or playing skittles, or some such thing, haven't we, Jasper?"

He turned in appeal to his friend, who nodded. "Yes," he agreed. "Either that, or we've been out hawking, you've not had time to do anything wrong."

"And have you spent any time in company with Cecily?" asked Hal gently.

Ned looked blank. "Well no," he agreed. "But she's been taken up with getting the house straight with Mary, so that I've barely seen her, except at meal times, haven't we, Jasper?"

"And I suppose then you've been full of tales of the chase, or games won?" suggested Hal.

Ned looked disconcerted. "Well, I can't find a lot of interest in how many dirty windows have been washed, or what lay at the bottom of a great chest," he said, a shade defensively.

"Oh, you think these great houses keep themselves clean, do you?" Hal asked.

"Well, no," agreed Ned, "but there are servants—"

"And who must direct the servants, and oversee their work?" interrupted Hal.

"Women's work," said Jasper quickly. "They have the eye for it."

"No, a responsible person's work," said Hal. "The running of an estate requires that all pull evenly, men and women, and that none sit at the side playing."

Jasper looked disconcerted, whilst Ned said truculently, "What, you would have me take a broom and sweep out the attics?"

"No, but I've no doubt there are a hundred things you could be doing to assist Guy. The garden appears to be in a terrible state," said Hal thoughtfully.

"You expect me to clip hedges and scythe grass?" asked Ned in horror.

"I am sure there are half a dozen gardeners," said Hal impatiently. "But, as you well know from your own estate management, all such good and worthy men require supervision. Guy cannot be everywhere at once, and there are only so many hours in the day. Naturally, he must attend to the farms first. However, if you are too genteel and exquisite for such assistance as you could with a modicum of intelligence give, then I do suggest you return home, where you can be of real use."

Jasper let out his breath. "That is a masterly set-down," he said with feeling. "No wonder they made you a Justice!"

Ned, his race red, looked ashamed. "Naturally, I'll be pleased to assist Guy in whatever way I can," he said stiffly. "I just wasn't aware he required help."

"Perhaps it might do you good to concentrate on another's troubles for a while, to put your own into perspective," said Hal. "In the meantime, once I've spoken again to Mr Durward here, I'll seek out Cecily, and talk to her."

"Will you, Hal?" asked Ned eagerly. "Can you make it right for me again?"

"I'm sure I can smooth over any difficulty, but you have to begin afresh, too. You must show an interest in her concerns, talk less about your favourite sports, and above all, spend a little time with her, without your good friend Jasper, and if possible, not mentioning him."

Chapter Seven

Whilst Hal was engaged with his brother and friend, Justin went to look for Giles Durward, a search that appeared fruitless until he came to the stables, where he finally found his quarry engaged in cuffing his groom. Giles stopped at Justin's look of amazement, saying, in a manner he couldn't stop from being defensive: "The damned young rascal has too long a tongue for my liking."

"I wonder you keep him then," said Justin, wondering privately why the lad stayed.

"Oh, he's been with me since he was a babe in arms," replied Durward. "His father served my father, that sort of thing. That's the trouble with having a good background, one has certain obligations, but you, of course, wouldn't understand such a notion."

"No," agreed Justin. "I find it difficult to understand

any obligation to ill-treat a servant. If any of mine and I don't agree, we part with self-respect retained on both sides."

"Yes, the noveau riche never did learn how to behave in under three generations, did they? But however, there's no riche with you, is there? How come you to bungle that so badly, Danvers? To be cut out by your own sister? I'll warrant Sir Henry is most pleased with his bargain! Wealthy bride to begin with, a vast dowry, and then an heiress within five years, and all it took was a push in the dark for her step-mother!"

Justin mastered the desire to hit him, and abandoned this form of sparring, which he judged the other to be an expert in. "I was looking for Cecily Armstrong," he said mendaciously. "Is she not in your company today?"

"No, she has just returned to the house, with a posy of flowers which I helped her gather by the lake," he replied curtly then, as Justin raised his brows, Giles laughed, adding: "Lord, how easily you ex-Puritans are taken in. Dear little Cecily is hardly my quarry, her dowry is too small, and rustic flowers are hardly my line."

"Your behaviour last evening gives that the lie," replied Justin mildly.

"My behaviour last evening was designed to make

Mistress Sophia every bit as jealous as it has done. She is in a perfect fury today, but will soon come to hand, once she realises little Cecily is not my object, merely a method of teaching her a lesson."

"A little hard on Cecily, surely?" Justin remarked.

"Not at all," he replied. "I've opened her eyes and widened her horizons for her. A desperate, dull life threatened the poor child, with that churlish bore, Ned Westwood. Why, she'd be driven to find a lover within three months, though I gather Sir Henry would fill that situation with alacrity. He has a liking for family females, I understand, and Cecily is nothing if not warm in his praises already. Mothers really do not teach their daughters a great deal these days, her head is full of how wonderful Hal is."

Wondering if it were Cecily who had been his informant of family affairs, or Guy in his cups, Justin gritted his teeth and asked: "So, you think you'll be successful in your wooing of Mistress Sophia. She'll have a pretty fortune if you can gain Master Benton's approval."

"'Tis already done, my good friend, this morning, whilst everyone was in church," he replied sarcastically. "I spoke to the old fool, and he was as encouraging as his type ever are! Well, I knew I couldn't fail, I mean, who else is there? Other than that clown of an inn-keeper at the Greyhounds, and the old fool has set his face against him. That's the trouble with spending your days in the pursuit of avarice, come the end of your life, you've nobody to leave it too." He stretched and yawned. "Yes, matters are working out very well, very well indeed. I'm glad we made the visit. I'll have Mistress Sophia and her fortune, and if you are very lucky, I'll let you draw up the settlements for me."

Justin bowed to hide his face of disgust. "I am honoured," he said ironically.

"Oh, I am not adverse to new blood," Durward replied magnanimously. "I've an attorney at home, of course, a crusty old fellow. But I hear you are something rather special, and should be able to get me the very best terms. I want free access to the money at once, of course."

"As I was saying, I am honoured, but alas, I am already retained by Master Benton," said Justin with satisfaction.

"Really, how provoking," sighed Durward. "But need that matter, I mean, surely 'tis all to the good? You'll know the terms of his will, in that case, I can make it worth your while above and beyond the usual fee."

"Regretfully, such practices are against the code of ethics," said Justin austerely. "But that aside, are you truly so sure of Mistress Sophia? From my observations, she is a spirited young woman, with ideas of her own in her head."

Durward laughed. "I like 'em high spirited," he replied. "It makes the breaking of 'em more enjoyable. You'll see, I'll tame Mistress Sophia in no time. Neither woman nor beast has ever withstood me!"

"I shall await events with great interest," said Justin, bowing again to hide his face. "In the meantime, I'll continue my quest for Mistress Cecily, if you'll excuse me."

"Oh aye, be off, my good fellow, don't let me detain you," he replied with a lordly air. "And if you should decide differently in that matter, let me know, I could make you a rich man."

Justin walked across the yard and into the house, shaking with a rare rage. He followed the passage and presently, after several twists, came into the Hall where Sophie was sitting, gazing from the window in an abstracted fashion. It was none of his business to advise her, but so full of wrath was he, that he crossed to her side. "Mistress Redcroft," he said softly. "May I speak to you on a private matter?"

"Mr Danvers, but of course," she replied, starting as from a daydream. She raised her eyes to his face, recollected he was Hal's brother-in-law and blushed rosily to think of her previous thoughts. Hal's wife was this man's sister, she must take great care. "How may I help you, sir?"

"I wish to help you, ma'am," he replied, sitting opposite her and speaking earnestly. "Hal—Sir Henry spoke earlier of you being incommoded by Mr Durward. He said—if you'll forgive the liberty of our discussing your affairs—that the young man had been importuning you to marry him, is that correct?"

"Yes," she replied, wondering what else Hal had said of her. "But I refused him very bluntly in the end."

"I greatly fear, ma'am, he means to marry you anyway," Justin replied.

She laughed. "He means to, Mr Danvers, but without my consent, he cannot."

"Madam, there are ways and means of getting a maid's consent to marriage, if the man is as unscrupulous as Durward appears to be. I greatly fear he means to have you by fair means or foul."

She returned his look, some of her bright colour fading. "Oh, how—how very horrible. Has he said so?"

"No, he didn't mention his method specifically, but his intentions came through in his general conversation. I warn you now, not to trust him at any costs. Recollect you are an heiress and the combination of your lovely face and large fortune will be irresistible to a man of no principle. He may hope to win you by fair means. But if you are too definite in your refusals, he may decide to take other, less pleasant measures."

"I assure you, his wooing isn't pleasant," she replied tartly.

"Then consider, ma'am, how unpleasant rapine may be," he replied swiftly.

She paled visibly. "He surely would not dare," she whispered.

"Mistress Redcroft, you are very unprotected," he said, as gently as possible. "Your guardian is a wealthy old man. If one as unscrupulous as Durward is determined upon a course of action, what possible opposition could he offer?"

"But surely public opinion, the scandal? Oh, he could not dare! Does he not think there would be an outcry?"

Justin glanced to her, pity in his eyes. "And that would damn you forever," he replied.

She looked appalled. "What must be done?" she asked numbly.

"'T'were best you were married immediately," replied Justin, and as she darted him an odd look, he added: "Marriage to another, a man you can like, must surely be your best protection."

"And what if no such man exists?" she replied.

Justin stared. "But he does," he replied. "Adam Blackwell. You like him, he is more than willing to marry you."

"My guardian will not countenance such a match," she retorted swiftly.

"Yes, I must talk with him," he replied. "But if I get him to consent, you must see, it's your best protection from such predatory beings as Durward."

"I see what you say," she agreed, "but I cannot marry Adam. I am fond of him, but marriage? No."

"Yet you must be married," said Justin, and it suddenly occurred to him that he was more insistent than was his want.

"No," she replied flatly. "Thank you for your concern, but I must take my chance. I cannot marry, unless my heart goes with it."

Justin frowned. "You seem very certain, Mistress Redcroft, and if this is the case, you must take care in your dealings with Giles Durward. At the moment, he is convinced he holds your fate in the palm of his hand. Disillusion him, and I cannot be answerable for the consequences."

"Play his game, you mean? Oh, do not think I could! Ha—he would think—I—I could not so dissemble," she stammered.

Justin darted her a sharp look, wondering if she stumbled over Hal's name, or if he'd misheard her. "I cannot urge you to this course of action too strongly," he said austerely. "If you are in the danger I believe you to be, you have little choice. However, I cannot force you, so I'll pressure you no longer, but instead seek your guardian."

He went from the room, leaving her prey to indecision. Part of her acknowledged what he said as true, there was in Giles Durward a ruthlessness that frightened her from the first time of their meeting, even as his strength attracted her. But another part of her mind said, this Justin Danvers is renowned as very shrewd, he has seen, or guessed, the attraction between Hal and

I. He suggests this course of action, that my behaviour might disgust Hal, and that he might think of me no more, might dismiss me as a flirtatious jade, and so go home to his wife, Justin's sister, thinking himself well rid of me.

As she sat thinking, Giles Durward entered, a smile creasing his lips as he saw her. His dark eyes suddenly lit with interest. "Well met, Mistress Sophia," he cried. "Have you forgiven me my slight?"

Still undecided, she was minded to err on the side of caution. "Indeed, yes, Mr Durward," she replied lightly. "For I did not take them seriously, knowing as I do, your admiration for little Cecily Armstrong."

"Tut-tut, kitty has claws, has she?" he replied, sweeping across the hall to stand close to her on the window seat, barring her escape again.

"Kitty?" she replied. "No, but a cat of a different colour, mayhap."

"I vow, my love, a man might keep you for a year, and not grow weary of your witty tongue," he said. "But take care it doesn't grow sharp!" Then, looking down at her, he tilted her chin, so that she was forced to look into his eyes. "Have no fear of pretty little Cecily Armstrong," he said in a different tone. "She is nothing to me. I want a woman to wife, not a pretty child."

"I have no fear of Cecily, but it seems she should have fear of you," she replied, holding his gaze, though she shuddered inwardly and longed to look away from the mixture of desire and cupidity she saw there. "If your attentions last night meant nothing, then I fear she is sadly led astray."

"Cecily led astray, nay," he laughed. "I tell you, I've enlivened her dull existence. A few kisses from a man who doesn't fumble over them, or smell of horses, brought her joy." Then, as her face mirrored her disgust, he bent his head swiftly, and gathered her into his arms, kissing her with an air of intense passion. "See, my lovely," he added, holding her close, as she, revulsed, struggled to break free from him. "I'll teach you not to fear my embrace either, but to cry out for it!"

A muffled squeak made him glance up, and in a second, Sophie was free. She dashed her trembling hand across her mouth, as if to wipe his kiss away in disgust, and turned in time to see Cecily, tears crowding to her eyes, rush back up the stairs.

A startled oath fell from Durward's lips, but the entrance of Hal forestalled any words.

"Good afternoon," Hal said politely, glancing from

Sophie's scarlet face, to Durward's countenance of annoyance. "My sister Mary begs me inform you, dinner is served. Have you seen Cecily?"

Tears filled Sophie's eyes, too, as under his cool gaze, she felt eternally shamed. "Cecily? She—she ran back upstairs. She—she is distressed, I believe."

"Distressed?" Hal repeated sharply. "Then I'd better go to her. Perhaps Mr Durward will be so good as to escort you into dinner?"

"Thank you, I need no escort," said Sophie, making hastily for the door. "Mistress Armstrong might need my help."

Hal, moving up the stairs, was aware of Durward's eyes on his back, but felt no inclination to acknowledge him. He found Cecily in her chamber, her head on the windowsill, as she sobbed her heart out. "Sweet Cecily, why do you weep?" he said at once, advancing into the room.

"Oh Hal," she cried, raising her head and looking at him through her tears. "Oh Hal, I've made such a mess of everything!"

"Haven't you, though," he agreed, coming to sit beside her.

"I thought if Ned could see that another man thought

me interesting, he might find more time for me, and not be forever with Jasper Durward," she confided, accepting the handkerchief he handed her, and quickly wiping her swollen eyes. "Only, instead of that, he told me that I was behaving like a jade, and that he'd not tolerate his betrothed talking to another man, and I was so angry at him, that I told him if that was his attitude, our betrothal was at an end, and that he had no right to lecture me anyway!"

"Well, that told him, didn't it," Hal agreed, patting her hand sympathically.

"It did, but do you know what he said then?"

Hal did, but judged it right to let her get it off her chest. "No, what?"

"He told me not to be so silly, and to get into such a state, but to tell him what was amiss so he could solve things. How like a man!"

"Indeed," soothed Hal. "So, did you tell him?"

"No, I did not," she cried. "Why, if he doesn't know, then I don't know if anything signifies anymore."

"I suppose," said Hal, hazarding a guess, "you were irked at his seeming indifference to you breaking off your betrothal?"

"He said not one word!" she cried, showing him how

successful he'd been. "But stood staring at me with his eyebrows all knitted. You know, the way he does."

"Oh yes," said Hal cleverly. "When he's dreadfully hurt by something."

"Dreadfully hurt?" she asked. "But he'd hurt me, by calling me those names."

"Which he would never have done, if he hadn't been very miserable. You see, he thinks you no longer love him, but have fallen for Giles Durward."

"That knave!" she cried. "I'd sooner die an old maid!"

"But, my dear, you've spent the weekend encouraging him," Hal objected.

"Only to teach Ned a lesson," she said, tears falling again. "But it didn't work, he was plainly glad to be rid of me. And as for Giles Durward—he says I am naught but a pretty child, with not enough fortune to tempt him. Odious man!"

"Odious man, indeed," he agreed. "But you, my poor silly. Why the tears? You still love Ned and he loves you, this is nothing but a lover's quarrel."

"No, it's not, Hal," she replied, really weeping again. "It goes much deeper than that. If Ned doesn't care enough to find out how I'm feeling, then there is no point in our betrothal."

"And if you don't care enough to find out how he is feeling, you'll never be married," Hal said bracingly. "Come, 'tis dinner time, come downstairs and kiss and make up."

"Oh Hal, I couldn't," she cried. "I can't face everyone looking like this, and I can't eat either!"

"No, perhaps not," he agreed, thinking of Giles Durward at his most sarcastic, making matters worse. "Look, it's stopped raining, slip out into the garden. I'll send Ned out to you, and you'll have to both talk to each other to get over this silly quarrel. Remember what Libby says: 'True love conquers all!' Now run along, I must return to Chawcester after dinner, and I want to know everything is right between you."

⚜

Chapter Eight

"Master Benton, can I speak with you?" Justin asked, coming into the parlour after dinner.

Edmund Benton sighed, for he'd been contemplating a snooze, but gave the other his attention.

"I thought I could take this opportunity, whilst Hal is talking to his brother, to bring a few points to your notice."

"Indeed, young man," he replied. "And have you found out yet if Robin was killed?"

"I must confess, I can prove nothing," said Justin. "But I am inclined to believe he was."

"You think so?" cried the Maltster. "Ha, I said as much! But do you know who did it?"

"I am pretty much convinced of the murderer," replied Justin. "But again, I have no proof, and so can say nothing until I do."

The older man nodded. "Aye, take away no man's character without due cause," he agreed. "Can you get proof?"

Justin shook his head, looking dissatisfied. "Nothing that will hold, not in a court of law. But this is by the by, I shall give you a full report tomorrow afternoon. I have two other people I must interview, before I can draw my conclusions. In the meantime, a more pressing matter. How is your money disposed this day?"

"My will?" asked the old man. "I've told you, Sophie gets it all if she weds at my bidding."

"And if she doesn't?"

"Then it goes to the Town Guild, every penny of it," he firmly replied.

"I see, and who would you have her wed?" asked Justin.

"Ah, there's the rub, at present there is nobody suitable."

"And if you were to be taken next week?" Justin asked. "How would it fall out then? Would Sophie have a guardian, and would he be empowered to choose her bridegroom?"

"Oh, indeed, that is all settled," said the old man comfortably. "My very good friend Alderman Chegleigh, he who I spoke of last evening, was named as Sophie's guardian, but his death at the end of last month left me in a quandary that I'd not been able to resolve. Until, that is, you and your brother-in-law called upon me yesterday. I was so impressed by your good sense and Sir Henry's unerring skill in handling Sophie, and convinced of your goodness of heart, that I, there and then, sent for Jonas Capel and had a fresh will made out. It had been troubling me, I must confess, I'd had it in my mind to pick a younger fellow, but then, as a masterstroke, I fixed upon the two of you, so that even if one of you should die, I'd not have to begin again."

"Hal and myself?" said Justin in astonishment. "But, forgive me, you barely know us!"

"I've spent enough time in your company to know you to be honest and honourable men," he replied quickly. "I am a merchant, sir, used to making swift judgements and decisions on the shake of a hand. A man doesn't get to my age without getting to know his fellows."

Justin was completely amazed, it was customary to ask a man to stand guardian, yet how could he intimate as much without offending the prickly merchant and appearing churlish. "For myself, Master Benton, I am honoured by the confidence you show in me, but I cannot speak for Sir Henry," he added with a shade of unease.

"Sir Henry is an excellent man, I am certain he'll raise no objection," said Edmund Benton, looking pleased with himself. "I was going to speak of it to you both tomorrow, as like as not, you know, it will never come to it, for I look to see Sophie safely married within weeks."

"Within weeks?" repeated Justin. "May I ask to whom?"

"Well, you know, I accepted your kinsman's hospitality on purpose, to get a look at Sir Henry's younger brother," he said, lowering his voice to a more confidential tone. "I cannot deny I was greatly impressed by Sir Henry, and Sophie never stopped talking of him. Well, with him being married, I thought, why not take a look at his younger brother, Ned Westwood, he might well be suitable."

"Ned Westwood is betrothed!" said Justin sharply.

The older man laughed cynically. "I doubt me if Sophie had been suited, that would have carried much weight! Sir Henry is a man of great sense, and one doesn't get as wealthy as he without looking out for his family's best interests. No, Ned would have been just right, but alas, he is nothing like Sir Henry! It wasn't just the handsome face, I told Sophie not to be so foolish as to expect every man to look like Sir Henry, but an uncouth, tongue-tied lad with naught to say for himself? I don't wonder Sophie wasn't impressed!"

"Ned and Cecily's marriage will be a love match," remarked Justin coldly.

"Aye?" said the Maltster in some amusement. "I heard your marriage was too! Love didn't serve you a good turn did it, my lad?"

"On the contrary," snapped Justin. "I would be nothing but for my wife."

"A wealthy nothing, though," he replied with a smile. "Nay, lad, don't get so fired up, I'm jesting with you. I admire your heart and your loyalty."

"You are still left without a suitable candidate for Sophie," said Justin pointedly.

"Aye, for I'm not much impressed by this Giles Durward. A man of straw, with his curled wig and his red-heeled shoes," agreed the Maltster. "Although, I said he might try."

"If you'll take my advice," said Justin. "You'll accept Adam Blackwell."

"No, never! That scurvy oaf? Not if my life depended

upon it!" he cried.

"He is a good man, a gentleman," said Justin. "I know he has no fortune to speak of, but he is sincerely attached to Mistress Sophia—"

"Sincerely attached to my money," he interrupted. "No, say no more, young man. I shall find someone, the Mayor has a nephew living in Oxford, true, he has six children, and his wife is but lately dead, but he might be the very one for Sophie."

"Sir, I tell you most urgently, that I believe Giles Durward has designs upon Mistress Sophia," Justin said, seeing he'd not listen.

"I am not a fool young man!" he replied. "I know that very well, most men that see Sophie do."

"Most men are not so unscrupulous as Durward!" Justin replied sharply.

"You think him unscrupulous, do you? Hmm. I don't know, but I am here, I shall be watching him." Master Benton said finally, considering Justin's words with true weight.

"You weren't there this morning, when he waylaid her on her return from church. Hal had to rescue her," Justin retorted in exasperation.

"Waylaid her on the return from church? Aye, he said

he'd try to woo her, and he failed! By heaven, I would that Sir Henry weren't a married man. He rescued her, did he? Well, that will have done him no disservice with Sophie."

"Sir Henry is married to my sister," said Justin sharply.

"I'd forgotten that. Your pardon, young man," he replied, looking a little shame-faced. "So, you are doubly connected with the Westwoods. How odd, for so will be the Armstrongs. A pity Guy Armstrong's brother was killed, he might have suited Sophie."

Seeing he'd get no more from him, Justin got to his feet. "Sir Henry and I are returning to Chawcester within the hour, sir, do you ride with us?"

"Yes indeed, Mr Danvers, always best to ride in cavalcade, even in these peaceful times. One never knows when they may be cut-purses about."

Reassured in this respect at least, Justin went off to find Hal. He was still with Ned and Cecily, who appeared to have made up their differences, but not entirely without some trouble.

"Then we are agreed, are we not," Hal was saying as Justin joined them, "that you both wish to remain betrothed?"

"Yes," said Ned, frowning fiercely.

"Cecily?" Hal glanced to her.

She sighed. "Yes," she said pettishly.

"You are certain?" he asked sharply. "You don't sound certain, if you are not sure, Cecily, we can put off your marriage."

"I still don't see why I should be taken to task for walking with a gentleman. If Ned is allowed friends, why should I not be?" she replied, disregarding this.

Ned looked appalled at this suggestion and said sharply, angry colour flooding his face: "Because Durward is no gentleman!"

"I do not think you'd be very happy if Ned's friend was a young lady, Cecily, so it follows that he will not be pleased that yours was a man," said Hal austerely.

"I only walked in the garden with him," she cried, reddening. "He helped me pick flowers."

"Pick flowers!" snarled Ned. "You little fool, he wasn't after picking blossoms!"

"Ned!" cried Hal, a warning note in his voice.

"How do you know?" she cried angrily. "Just because you don't care to walk with me, because you aren't interested in the same things as I, does it mean no man can be? Giles knows a lot about flowers. He knew all the names and most of the herbs, too, his mother taught him!"

"I think perhaps, Ned, it might be as well for you to come to Chawcester with us," Hal intervened as Ned grew angrier. "For it seems you'll only quarrel further if you are left together."

"What and leave her to Durward?" cried Ned. "Never!"

"You're a dog in the manger, Ned Westwood, so you are!" cried Cecily, incensed. "You don't want me yourself, but you're damned if you'll let another have me either!"

"Who says I don't want you," he shouted. "By God, I've wanted you everyday for the past eighteen months! Is it my fault my father died?"

"You've a funny way of showing how much you want me, by avoiding my company!" she retorted, tears filling her eyes.

"By God!" he cried, crashing his fist into the palm of his other hand. "Don't try me too far, woman!"

Obedient to the signal in Hal's eyes, Justin took Ned's arm. "Come, Ned, walk with me to the stables," he said quickly. "My horse is going lame, or so that groom of Guy's insists, you'll be able to tell me if the man's the fool I think him."

"Cecily, Cecily, what are you about?' said Hal shaking her arm a little as Justin and Ned walked away. "You little fool, don't you see how hard you are riding him?" Then, as she stared at him innocently, he laughed awkwardly. "No, I don't suppose you do, either." He scratched his chin in an embarrassed manner. "Ned has been raised a gentleman, my dear. His sense of honour demands that until you are married, he may not touch you beyond the normal courtesies of a betrothal. He is, however, a passionate man, too, and one very much in love. He must, therefore, walk a tightrope of desire, which by my guess troubles him greatly. Thus, you find him exhausting himself with hunting and exercise and keeping company with you only when you are chaperoned. Lest his tightly reigned-in desires betray him into some insult."

Her gaze faltered and fell as he spoke, and a deep blush spread from her neck up to her cheeks. "Oh," she said. "So it's not that he is tired of me, more that…"

"He fears to be alone with you, lest he gives way to his baser instincts," concluded Hal. "I assure you, my dear, once you are married, he'll seldom leave your side."

She bit her bottom lip and peeped up at him bashfully. "I—I beg pardon for being so silly, and for embarrassing you," she whispered.

"You aren't silly," he said, giving her a quick affectionate hug. "You're just young and innocent, but I pray you, and heed me well, if you wish to remain so, abjure Durward's company. He is not a good and honourable man."

She nodded. "He frightens me," she confessed. "But I—I don't always know how to refuse him."

"Stay close by Mary at all times, she'll be able to deal with him," he replied. "And now I must find her and take my leave, if we are to get back to Chawcester before nightfall."

They went together to find his sister, and whilst Cecily took the baby to his nurse, Hal enlightened his sister as to what had been going on. He also insisted that she instruct her young sister-in-law more fully, and watch her more closely.

Finally, Hal fetched up in the stable yard as the heat of the day began to wane, giving them the promise of a pleasant ride through the cool of the evening.

"Ah, Sir Henry, are you come at last?" Master Benton, who was already astride his sturdy cob, cried. Your brother-in-law is in a fuss over his hack, the groom says its hock is swollen, but young Mr Westwood says not."

"It's merely a sprained hock, Hal," said Ned, straightening up and brushing his hand on the seat of his breeches. "Don't push him, Justin, and all will be well, although you should complain to your horse coper."

"Well, I will," Justin said, putting his foot in the stirrup, and sliding easily into the saddle. "But I doubt me it'll do any good. We hired from the Greyhound, and the innkeeper dislikes us mightily."

"Will you take a cup of this excellent wine that Durward has kindly brought us, to speed us on our way, Sir Henry?" asked Master Benton, offering him a stirrup cup.

"No, I thank you," replied Hal. He suppressed a groan as Sophie appeared. Her gown outlined her trim figure, leaving little to the imagination. Guy swiftly helped her into the saddle, and as farewells were exchanged, she brought her horse alongside Hal's, following Master Benton and Justin from the yard. He glanced back over his shoulder, reassured to see Cecily standing close to Mary, with Ned next to her. He had a fleeting glimpse of Giles Durward's face, and then the avenue curved away.

"So, Sir Henry, you've been avoiding me," Sophie opened the conversation quietly, her eyes on the figures in front, who were deep in a monetary discussion.

"No, ma'am," he replied. "I have been too busy to even think of you." That was the answer. Kill her mad infatuation with cruelty. Never mind that it hurt her, that it crucified him, he had to be cruel to be kind to them both.

"That was not kind, Hal," she turned to look at him with tears swimming in her great violet eyes. "Why should I be kind?" he replied, his voice hard. "You are determined to be foolish, therefore I cannot risk being kind."

"I am not determined to be foolish. I can't help it anymore than you can," she replied, laughing a little. "Do you think I wanted to fall in love with you? Do you think I am pleased that every man I now see compares unfavourably with you?"

"I neither know or care," he replied harshly.

Tears trickled down her nose. "Then you might have a little pity, if nothing else," she whispered.

His heart ached at the sight of her tears, but he steeled himself. "Pity? Why should I have pity? Your suffering is self-inflicted," he replied roughly. "I have given you no encouragement."

"No, not even a kiss to steal my heart away?" she

countered. "Did you not hold me in your arms for a few seconds that felt like eternity?"

The recollection of it came to him, firing him with desire for her lips again, filling him with a longing to take her in his arms. She was right, those few seconds had felt like eternity, he could have stayed locked in her embrace forever. Angry with the flood of uncontrollable feelings, he snapped: "Madam, because you threw yourself at me, I am not to blame. I am sorry you suffer, but I tell you plainly, you brought it upon yourself."

"You might tell me that you suffer too," she replied wistfully. "It would help to ease my pain if I thought I didn't suffer alone."

"I don't see how knowing another suffers eases your pain. It might heal hurt pride, I suppose," he said coldly.

"Oh Hal, how you twist the knife," she cried. "I never thought you could be so cruel."

"One of us must apply some common sense," he replied, though his heart cried out at her words.

She wiped away her tears with the back of her hand and he felt his wretchedness complete. He, that had comforted so many women, couldn't even offer a crumb to the most precious being of his heart. He held out a clean handkerchief.

"As well I had another," he said curtly. "Cecily had the last. Another foolish wench."

She wiped her eyes and held the kerchief to her nose, inhaling the smell of him that was on it, treasuring the fact it was his. "Is that how you see me?" she whispered humbly.

"Yes," he replied harshly. "A troublesome, foolish wench with neither sense nor decorum. If you were my daughter, I'd beat you."

"Your daughter," she laughed. "You are but seven years my senior, I could never be your daughter."

"Sister then," he replied. "I have a sister about your age, who was in my charge until she was married. If she'd behaved so badly I'd have beaten her."

A smile trembled on her lips. "I think I might quite enjoy being beaten by you," she said saucily.

He threw her a look of outrage, as he recognised he, too, would enjoy mastering her. "Ma'am," he said ominously, "hold your tongue."

"How old are your children?" she asked, ignoring this command.

"Harry is four," he replied, bewildered by this sudden change of topic, "and the baby, Francis, is but a month old."

"And you have been married five years?" she continued.

"Very nearly five," he replied. "Five years next week."

"Shall you be at home with your wife by then?" she asked, her voice sounding desolate.

"Pray God," he replied, his tone heartfelt, as he thought of the security of Westwood. "The Sessions close tomorrow, I have but to visit Chipping Barbury on Wednesday, and I should be home before Friday."

"Will she be there, eagerly waiting for you?" she made her demand, almost as if she had to know.

"It is her custom if I am expected," he replied. He wished to show her that he was happily married, yet he felt a measure of disloyalty to Libby, to be discussing her with another woman.

"Do you love her?" Sophie blurted out the question, her voice rising, so that Justin glanced back curiously.

"She is my dearest love," he replied, as if repeating a catechism. "She gives meaning to my life, sense to my days, joy to my existence, without her I could not live."

She bit her lip, and looked away across the sundrenched fields, where the corn grew thick and green.

"You think me very impertinent," she said, and it was a statement, not a question.

"I think you very foolish, very unhappy, and I am sorry for it," he replied more gently. "Sorrier yet if I have inadvertently added to your misery, I beg pardon for it."

"Don't!" she cried, and then as Justin glanced back again, she managed a wobbly smile. "Don't apologise, I beg. I have no doubt my malady will be of short duration, your physic, employed with such ruthlessness, is most efficacious."

"I am glad of it," he replied,, but his heart was heavy. "I wish you a speedy recovery, Mistress Sophia."

"Oh, I've no doubt of it," she countered. "My guardian has yet another physic, a husband, that should complete the cure, don't you think?"

His heart gave a queer lurch, and his voice wasn't quite steady as he replied. "A complete cure, I wish you joy, Ma'am, I wish you joy."

She nodded her head in a way that was almost queenly, and spoke not another word. Presently, as the way grew wider, by common consent they drew alongside the others, and the conversation became more general, with a discussion of the beauty of the evening, and the effects of a long ride on unaccustomed older bones. They parted in the High Street, outside Master Benton's smart town house, Justin and Hal proceeding to the bottom of the narrow street and the Greyhound, there to while away the remainder of the evening in a discussion of all they had so far discovered.

Chapter Nine

Hal awoke at dawn from the grip of a nightmare, clutching his pillow to him. However much he was be able to control his thoughts by day, in his dreams they ran amuck, leaving him feeling exhausted and angry with himself.

He unwound the sheets and got from the bed sweating, and crossed to the window to lean out in the fresh morning air. The yard lay silent and glistening in the early morning dew, he rested his head on the sill and tried desperately to rid his thoughts of Sophia. He was shocked at the extent of how completely she possessed his mind. Having never been in love before, he was unprepared for the ordered calm of his life to be so upset, and rather dismayed to find how he was no different to any other man. He clung to thoughts of Libby like an anchor, yet even as he did so, he reluctantly recognised that his love for Libby, although firm and strong, had nothing like the earth-shattering feelings that he felt for this girl he'd met two days ago. His only consolation in all this was that he could walk away from the situation. By tomorrow morning, he could be finished in Chawcester. He need never set foot in the town again, certainly not before Mistress Sophia Redcroft was safely married.

It was at this point, that Sophie ran into the yard, tears running down her pale cheeks, a cloak clutched on over a nightgown. She hesitated, glancing up, and espying him, cried: "Hal! Oh Hal, thank God you are risen! Hal, Uncle Edmund is dead!"

"Dead!" he repeated in astonishment. "Master Benton?'

"Yes," she cried, her voice breaking. "Dead!"

"Good God!" he exclaimed, unable to believe this. "You are certain?"

She nodded, tears coursing down her cheeks, so that he was forced to think quickly. "Er—come—come up here, I'll wake Justin," he said blankly, unable to think of what to do or say.

Justin, however, had been roused by the sound of voices and was at his door as Hal knocked.

"What's amiss?" he asked tersely. "I thought I heard Mistress Sophia's voice."

"Yes, she said Master Benton is dead," Hal repeated blankly, as if he still couldn't comprehend it.

"Master Benton," Justin echoed in amazement. "Never!"

"So she—ah, here she is now. Do join me in the parlour, Justin," Hal suggested with a doubtful glance at the sobbing girl, as other doors began to open and guests along the corridor looked out to see the cause of the noise.

"Yes, yes, I'll just throw some clothes on," he agreed. "You try to calm her."

Hal took her hand. "Come Sophie," he soothed, leading her into the parlour. "Do try to be calm, and tell me what has happened."

"Oh, Hal," she cried, flinging herself against his chest as he shut the door on prying eyes. "Oh Hal, Uncle Edmund is dead."

"Yes, so you said," he agreed, patting her back gingerly, conscious that he was clad only in his nightshirt and that he wanted her very much. "How is he dead? Are you sure he is dead?"

"Oh yes," she replied. "Do you remember him complaining of how stiff he was, and how bad his rheumatism was last night, as we rode home?"

"Yes, now you mention it, I think I do," he agreed, although he had, in fact, attended to very little of the conversation, his thoughts being full of her. He found he was unable to resist stroking the hair back from her face as he added: "Didn't he say he was getting too old to ride out so far, and you teased him about getting a coach?"

"Yes," she said, catching her breath on a sob. "Yes, so I did. Well, when we parted, you went on to the Greyhound, but Uncle Edmund really didn't feel well. He stumbled getting from his horse, and Peter had to help him into the house and up the stairs. I fetched him some wine, but he said it tasted odd, and stuck in his throat, so Nance and I helped him to bed. I wanted to send for Master Cresswell, the apothecary, but Uncle Edmund wouldn't hear of it. He said he was merely exhausted, and he'd feel better in the morning. He took a little brandy wine, and I left him to sleep."

Tears splashed down her face again as she remembered it, and he held her close. "Now, now, don't cry," he soothed. "You did your best, if he didn't want the apothecary, you could hardly argue, could you?"

She shook her head, leaning it against his shoulder. "Oh Hal, I am so thankful I've you to come to," she whispered. "That I don't have to face this alone." She gazed up into his handsome face. "You don't know what it means to me to have you here, to feel you hold me close."

He returned her look, half-mesmerised in his longing to kiss her. He almost bent his head, but in time heard Justin's hand on the door.

"So you put him to bed, and left him," he said, loosening her hold a little. "What next? Ah, Justin, come sit with Mistress Sophia, that I might dress, if you please," he added as Justin entered, partially clothed, and carrying his hat, coat and boots.

"No, Hal, don't go," she cried, clutching hold of him. "Please don't leave me!"

"I shall not leave you," he soothed. "I shall just go into my chamber to get dressed. I'll leave the door open, that I might still hear you."

"Come Sophie," Justin took her hand and led her to a cushioned settle, going to pour her a cup of wine from the previous evening. Hal hastily departed into his chamber, saying: "Continue with the story, Sophie. If you remember, Justin, Master Benton felt unwell last evening on our ride home."

Justin nodded, pressing the wine into Sophie's trembling fingers, and went to pull on his boots.

She took a sip, and looked across to the door, through which Hal had disappeared, realising with astonishment, that by the placing of a mirror, she could clearly see him as he stripped off his damp nightshirt. Suppressing a gasp, she said unsteadily, "I— I slept ill. I had bad dreams, and then was wakeful, so I slipped along to see how Uncle Edmund did."

"At what time was this?" asked Justin, as Hal vigorously sluiced his head and torso with cold water.

"I do not know, I cannot be sure. No, wait, the Abbey clock struck the hour. I think it was three, but it may have been four—I wasn't listening."

"I heard the Abbey clock at four," called Hal, towelling his hair dry. "It was beginning to get light."

"Then it must have been three, it was quite dark."

"Quite right, no moon," called Justin, wandering over to the window as he shrugged on his coat and smoothed his cravat. "I remarked upon it, Hal. Mistress Sophia, how was your Uncle Edmund?"

"I wished I'd looked closely," she replied, tears trickling down her cheeks again. "I thought him sleeping soundly, so I only looked in on him."

"Never mind," Justin turned from the window, saw the same view of Hal as she did, and darted her a sharp glance. Sophie had her head down, her face in her hands. He walked round to stand in front of her. "You couldn't have known. And this morning?"

"I awoke with the headache," she replied dully. "I got up to get a tisane, and thought Uncle Edmund might care for one. I took mine in the still room and carried his to his chamber." Tears almost suspended her voice. "He was lying back on his pillows. At first I thought him dozing, then, then I—I realised—"

"Yes, yes, don't dwell upon it," Hal entered sketchily attired, his shirt unbuttoned, in his stocking feet, his waistcoat and coat under his arm. "Are my boots there, Justin," he asked, "and my hat?"

"Yes," Justin replied, picking up both articles. "You are hopeless, Hal, scattering your clothes all over the place, if there is no Libby to tidy up behind you. Look, here is your cravat."

"Oh good," he replied, buttoning his shirt. "I was wondering what I'd done with it. Pour us both a glass of wine, Justin. Sophie, can you continue? You found Uncle Edmund dead in his bed. Was he cold, were the covers disturbed? Cast to the floor perhaps? Was there any sign of a struggle?"

"No, none," she replied, shaking her head. "He was exactly as we'd left him the night before. He hadn't moved at all, but he was cold, stone cold."

"Died early on then," remarked Justin quietly, handing Hal his boots.

"So it would seem," he agreed. "And yet you say, Sophie, he was taken ill as soon as you got home?"

"Yes," she said tearfully. "Don't you remember him saying how his rheumatism was bad, that all his joints were stiff and aching?"

Hal, who could remember little beyond the torment of her words and the turmoil of his own emotions, nodded his head. "I do recall something of that sort."

"So do I," said Justin. "It was as we neared Chawcester; his horse faltered a little, and he said how weary he felt. He said he was too old for riding here and there, and Mistress Sophia said he must buy a coach, and travel in style to her wedding."

"Yes," said Hal, as tears slipped down Sophie's cheeks again. "I remember that. And by the time you got home he was very ill?"

"We parted in the High Street," said Justin. "Did you

ride to the stables?"

"No, they are in Avon Street at the back," she said. "Tom came running to help me down, and Uncle Edmund got from his horse. It was then he seemed to stumble. He said his legs wouldn't work, they were heavy. Then Peter came from the house and helped him straight upstairs to bed. Oh, I should have insisted on Master Cresswell coming!" she cried. "If only Master Cresswell had been there."

"He may not have been able to do anything," Justin said in a soothing tone, helping Hal into his coat and picking up both hats.

"Come," said Hal, taking his. "We shall go and see. Did you raise the whole house?"

"No, no!" she replied. "I only told Peter and said to send for Master Cresswell."

"Then let us hope we are first on the scene," Justin said, knowing from experience an apothecary would disturb everything.

In the event, they were first, Master Cresswell appearing some fifteen minutes later. Sophie was firmly despatched to dress by Justin, whilst he and Hal took a good look at the body.

"Rigor has set in," said Hal, standing at the foot of the bed and thinking at the vagaries of fate. Only last evening, this had been a fine, vigorous man, well in control of his life, and the lives of many people. Now he was nothing but an empty shell. He had passed on, leaving his concerns to others.

"Yes, but look how the teeth are clenched," said Justin, who was by the head of the bed. "This man died in great pain. Yet, he made no movement, none of his coverlets are disturbed, he has not thrashed about in agony."

"Pray God it was that quick," said Hal shuddering. "One terrible pain, perhaps, and that was all. A heart attack, most likely."

"Yes," said Justin doubtfully. "Yes, perhaps."

"You don't think so?" asked Hal.

"Well, I am no expert," Justin replied. "But there is no blueness. I am certain Rupert Gillings, my neighbour—you know, the apothecary in Adamsholme. He told me there was a blueness under the nails in heart failure, when I was talking to him about sudden death some months ago."

"He was but a student of medicine," Hal reminded him.

"That is why he is but an apothecary, but he'd studied abroad, too. However, Master Cresswell should be able to tell us more."

"What are you thinking of, foul play?" asked Hal abruptly.

"It passed through my mind," Justin replied bluntly. "I spoke to Master Benton yesterday afternoon, saying how worried I was, though, in truth, most of my worry was for Mistress Sophie."

"Why?" asked Hal.

"Until he reassured me, I thought her likely to be left penniless, unless she married at once, but he had made provision for her by naming guardians."

"Did he indeed, that is fortuitous," said Hal nodding. "But you think now you were wrong, and he was the one in danger?"

"I don't know," sighed Justin. "How can one be sure? 'Tis, 'tis merely that it doesn't smell right."

Hal nodded gloomily. "I know what you mean, but look, Justin, there's no proof either way. We can't prove Robin Tripp was killed either. So let us just abandon the whole thing, and leave it all to Mistress Sophia's new guardians. Let sleeping dogs lie, before we do any harm."

Justin darted him an odd look, it was unlike Hal to be so eager to abandon something begun. "I'd like to, Hal," he replied. "But unfortunately, as you and I are Mistress Sophia's guardians, I fear it will be impossible."

"What!" cried Hal, in a voice of incredulity, unable to believe fate could play such a trick upon him.

"It seems Master Benton called his man of law to him Saturday after we talked, and made you and I Sophie's guardians. He fully intended to explain, and beg pardon, but time has caught him out."

"He cannot do it!" cried Hal. "He must ask our consent. I cannot have this charge!"

"It is certainly unusual," agreed Justin. "And had you been consulted, you could indeed have refused, but now we are put in a difficult position."

"Difficult? Damnable!" cried Hal wrathfully.

Justin eyed him narrowly. "Why such heat, Hal?" he asked. "Granted, it's an imposition, but it need not worry us unduly. I, for my part, told the old man I was honoured."

"Then you can deal with the matter, for I refuse,"

Hal snapped, seeing his desire for escape eluding him. "I leave here first thing tomorrow morning, and I don't intend to return."

"What are you running from?" asked Justin saliently.

"Why do you assume I am running?" he snapped. "Just because I don't care to have charge of a hoyden of a girl laid upon me—"

"Master Cresswell is here," Sophie entered, freshly gowned in a dull colour, her eyes swollen from weeping, tears welling in them reproachfully at Hal's words.

"Then we'll leave him to his findings," said Hal hastily.

"Do you go ahead with Mistress Sophia, Hal, I'll stay and talk with the apothecary," said Justin.

"I've told Mary the cook to see to some breakfast," Sophie said, leading the way down the staircase.

She stopped as she began the lower stair and Hal above her drew almost level. "Why do you call me a hoyden?" she asked softly.

"I didn't mean you to hear," Hal replied, looking embarrassed, for such a direct attack was not what he was expecting.

"But I did hear. It hurt me. I am not a hoyden," she said bluntly.

"Ah, here is Master Cresswell, I make no doubt," said

Hal hastily, as the apothecary in his long gown came to the foot of the stairs.

"Sir Henry, I am honoured to make your acquaintance, though sad to do so on such a melancholy occasion," the man said, bowing low. "Poor neighbour Benton, a good friend who'll be sadly missed. Mistress Sophia, you have my condolences."

"I was not aware we'd met," said Hal, as Sophie gave the man her hand.

"Strictly speaking we've not, Sir Henry," he replied. "Thomas Cresswell at your service, Master Apothecary. I had the great pleasure to be in the court when you sent that rogue Jack Datchet to the Assizes. I was glad to see the fellow get what he deserved, if I might be allowed to say so."

"You may," said Hal. "I am relieved to hear some of the people of this town believe in justice. I'd been given to understand my decision was not popular."

"Adam Blackwell," nodded the man. "He's a fool! None but he had any faith in Datchet, but because he'd fought with his father for the King—"

"It was because the man had fought for the King, I recommended his life be spared," replied Hal. "But for that, by any stretch of the imagination, he should have faced the gallows."

"Indeed, the fellow may count himself lucky, but I mustn't detain you. I'll go about my melancholy business. I shall be happy to report my findings presently."

"Odious man," snapped Sophie as they made the sanctuary of the parlour. "Oh, how I hate him and the smell of physic which clings to his gown."

"He can't help that," sighed Hal.

"He can help being an odious, toadying, spying fellow," she replied tartly. "And you've still not said why you called me a hoyden."

"I was angered and spoke out of turn," Hal replied quietly, seeing she'd not leave the subject. "I didn't mean it, but spoke in the heat of the moment. I beg pardon if I hurt your feelings, you are plainly not a hoyden."

"By heaven, that's a handsome apology," she cried staring. "Do you always admit your faults freely and comprehensively?"

"If it is merited," he replied, then, as she made a comical face, he laughed, saying: "Why is it I sound so old and so like my Aunt Margery when I speak to you?"

"Because you always try to lecture me," she replied promptly. "You are so intent on convincing yourself that you have no feelings for me, and telling me I am mistaken in mine, that you end up sounding like an old woman."

He glanced to her, half-exasperated, half-laughing, as he tacitly acknowledged the truth of this, then he sobered. "Sophie, who'd want to do harm to your Uncle?" he asked abruptly.

"Uncle Edmund? None, he was well respected," she replied at once.

"He'd turned off no thieving servant? He had no grasping rivals?" he asked.

"No, we've had all our people for years," she replied, frowning, reviewing the household. "As for rivals, yes, he had them in the town, on the council, but none ready to kill him! Do you think him murdered, then?"

"Yes— no—I cannot be sure," he replied. "Some things seem to suggest it, others make me think I've windmills in my head."

She laughed and then wept piteously. "I shouldn't be laughing," she explained. "I can't seem to believe Uncle Edmund is dead."

"No, it is difficult," he agreed. "And as for laughing, don't be foolish, your guardian liked to hear you laugh, that won't change because he is dead." Then, as she continued to weep, he thought of the sure method of diverting a weeping female. "Sophie, you spoke of a tisane earlier for the headache, could you brew one for me, my head aches damnably this morning."

Chapter Ten

Master Cresswell looked shocked, blowing out his full cheeks as he finished a rather cursory examination. "'Tis most likely his heart," he pronounced. "Master Benton had trouble before, he was of a 'choleric' disposition. I cupped him regularly."

"Yes," said Justin. "But shouldn't there be some signs, if it was heart failure?"

"No, not necessarily," he replied, affronted. "My good friend had been taking my sovereign remedy for his heart for the past year."

"And that is?" asked Justin patiently.

"It is a secret recipe," the man replied.

"Nothing is secret in a court of law," said Justin. "I don't demand all the ingredients, just the main ones."

The apothecary looked outraged. "Are you threatening me, Mr Danvers? If so, I shall seek the advice of my friend Sir Henry Westwood—"

"Who is my brother-in-law," concluded Justin sharply. "He will advise you to answer my questions, if you've nothing to hide."

The man goggled at him for a few moments, then muttered under his breath about 'jumped up attorney's clerks', but finally, as a spark lit in Justin's eyes, admitted the main component to be digitalis.

"Digitalis? Foxglove?" asked Justin. "Yes, yes, I see. Tell me, if he was given an overdose of this—"

"I am quite specific about doses, Mr Danvers!" the apothecary interrupted.

"Yes, I am sure you are. But, if by accident, or design, Master Benton were given more?"

"What are you suggesting? Poisoning?" cried the man, his face suddenly pale. "I wasn't here, I can't tell."

"But would there be any signs if he were given more of his remedy?" asked Justin patiently.

"Well, I suppose, he'd look much as he does," said the apothecary reluctantly.

"But no disturbing of the coverlets. I mean, he looks just as if he were struck," said Justin. "Isn't there usually discomfort first?"

"No, often it's one massive pain," sighed the man.

"Are you suggesting Mistress Sophia poisoned him?"

"No, not at all!" said Justin quickly. "I'm merely suggesting that he may have been given something—"

"Well, if it was digitalis, it wasn't long before," interrupted the apothecary. "It takes less than an hour to work. And if he was given an overdose, then he probably would have vomited it back up."

Justin nodded, as he finally got the information he required. "Well, that clears that up. Only, what would you say had killed him?"

"I cannot say, not for certain," he replied quickly. "I am only an apothecary, not a physician."

"Had he seen a physician?" asked Justin, with a sigh.

"I believe he consulted Doctor Douay, the French physician. It was he who said Master Benton's heart was affected," said the apothecary, with the air of a man washing his hands of any responsibility.

"Then I'd best speak to him," said Justin. "Has he been summoned?"

"He has been, but I doubt he'll come," said the man. "The great Dr Douay doesn't attend. One must seek him out. He is at the Sign of the Golden Key."

"Ah, yes, I know it," said Justin. "Well, if there's nothing more I can do here, I'll accompany you down to report to Sir Henry."

Hal was soon found. He was distastefully sipping a tisane, and he listened as patiently as Justin had done to all the apothecary's huffing and puffing and evasions. He finally dismissed the man with the reminder that he should hold himself ready to speak to the constable should this prove to be a suspicious death.

"Though, how we'd prove such a thing, I've no idea," Hal remarked, as the apothecary hurried thankfully away. The maid brought them a tankard of ale apiece and some bread and ham, and they sat down to breakfast.

Justin nodded gloomily. "It's exactly the same as with Robin Tripp. I've the liveliest suspicions, but until we can obtain some sort of proof, they must remain that."

"What we need to do," said Hal, drinking his ale thoughtfully, "is to panic the murderer—if we have a murderer—a little—to make him come out into the open. Only if he thinks he is likely to be discovered, is he likely to make a mistake."

"He's not likely to do so, is he?" asked Justin. "This murderer— if we have a murderer—thinks he is so clever, that none will ever discover him."

"Hmm, well, I just wish we were a hundred miles from here," said Hal, getting to his feet. "And now I must go. I've to be in court for ten-thirty."

"Won't you take some breakfast first," asked Justin. "It can't be that late, surely."

"'Tis gone nine, and I must shave and make myself ready," Hal replied. "Besides, I'm not hungry, I'll meet you back at the inn this evening."

"It seems to me," called Justin, as Hal hurried from the chamber, "that you must be love-sick, you've so little appetite."

Left alone, Justin sat for some while over his meal. He was trying to decide upon the best thing to do, and after much thought, finally came to the conclusion that he should proceed as planned yesterday. He'd see both Wat Rose and Will Greenway, and then persuade Hal to join him to meet with the French physician. Justin had very limited French, whereas Hal spoke it like a native after all his years in France, he'd be able to understand so much more.

His decision made, Justin took his leave of Sophie, telling her of his destination and impressing upon her the need to be circumspect.

His first task was to find Will Greenway. For, he reasoned, that Wat Rose would probably need some hours to sleep off the drink of the previous night. Sophie had told him that Will Greenway had a yard a short distance from Master Benton's wharf, which was behind the house. A cooper by trade, Will's hut backed onto the river, and as Justin knocked and entered the hut, Will laid the last blow on a band of iron and kicked the barrel through a gap in the wall designed for that purpose and into the river below.

"Will Greenway?" asked Justin, as the barrel hit the water with a splash.

"Who wants him?" replied the man curtly, throwing his hammer to one side and picking up a stave to examine it.

"I am Justin Danvers, attorney at law," he replied. "Master Benton, the late Master Benton, bade me come here to Chawcester to look into his journeyman's death."

"Master Benton is dead?" asked the cooper slowly.

"He died this morning of an apoplexy," said Justin.

"Rest his soul," said the man crossing himself. "Why, I only spoke to him Friday last, about these here barrels."

"Life's a chancy thing," agreed Justin. "Did he speak to you about Robin Tripp?"

"Only to say how he missed him, like," said the brawny fellow slowly. "He said he'd not realised how old he were getting, but that now he didn't have Robin to run his errands, he felt his age. And I said t'were a pity Saul Makepiece had been so unsuited to his trade, and Master Benton, he said he didn't regret him above half, and that pretty soon Davy Throstle would be old enough to be of real use to him."

"Davy Throstle? That's one of Master Benton's apprentices, isn't it?" asked Justin. "Who is Saul Makepiece?"

"Another of 'em," said the cooper. "Master Benton always took a new apprentice once a year. He always had done, ever since the war ended. Robin Tripp had finished his time and became a journeyman, the 'prentice Master Benton took the year after him died, when he were but a lad, of the green sickness he did, then came Saul Makepiece. Two years younger than Robin, he were, and due to finish his time this Easter. Only, Master Benton wouldn't keep him. Didn't trust him, mind—not many did."

"But I've heard nothing of this previously," cried Justin in dismay. "Master Benton made no mention of this to me!"

The cooper looked surprised. "Well, it all happened at Easter," he said in his slow way. "Happen, he never gave a thought to it. Saul finished his term, Master Benton presented him with a shovel as he always do, and that were the last any of us saw of him. He took up his pack and were last seen crossing King Henry's bridge, going up country."

"But the fellow might have held a grudge," exclaimed Justin, in dismay.

"Don't see it," said the cooper, rubbing his bristly chin. "A master ain't obliged to take on a 'prentice, some do, some don't."

"But there may have been a quarrel," said Justin. "There must have been a reason for Master Benton not keeping him on. You yourself said not many trusted him, why?"

"Blamed if I know," the man replied, looking surprised. "T'weren't that he ever did aught that I know of, t'were more that beside young Robin, he cut an ill figure. Robin were a slender, golden lad. Saul, he were short and stubby and cross-grained."

"Even more of a reason," said Justin in exasperation. "Don't you see? This Saul Makepiece may well have wanted to kill Robin and get even with Master Benton."

"Well, that do seem mortal wicked somehow," said the cooper looking bewildered. "I thought Robin's death were an accident, but if it weren't—" His slower wits tried to keep pace. "I'm not a-saying Saul weren't that bad—he were—well, he were just sneaky-like."

"Like a snake," suggested Justin. "To creep through the grass, strike and be off?"

"Aye, that sort of thing," agreed the cooper dubiously. "But I tell you, Saul Makepiece hasn't been seen since Easter."

"And Robin Tripp was killed in May," said Justin. "I'll take my guess he's not many miles away."

"Well, there be a Master Maltster in Malaford, so he can't have gone there, and there are several in Chipping Barbury, but I'm not sure about Eggsfield, nor yet Adamsholme." He glanced to his bundle of staves. "Is that all you be wanting, sir?"

"Hmm? Oh, no, no, I'm sorry. You've just opened up the possibilities enormously. No, I came to ask you if you saw aught on the night of the fire dance, when Robin Tripp was killed."

"Saw aught?" the man repeated. "Well, I saw him leap the flames, like, and I saw him die." He shuddered. "It finished me, I can tell 'ee! I won't leap again, not for ten pounds I wouldn't."

"I can't say as I blame you," said Justin thoughtfully.

"It can't have been a pretty sight."

"It wasn't!" said the man with fervour. "'Orrible it were, and Rob screaming out in agony." He shook his head. "Terrible, terrible!"

"But it was an accident, as far as you saw?" asked Justin.

"I never thought it were anything else," said the cooper, looking blank. "Be it murder, then?"

"Master Benton suspected so," said Justin. "It is possible. Did you actually see him jump?"

"Well no, t'were the smoke, see," said the cooper frowning. "I saw him jump both other times, but just as Robin were about to jump, the wind changed, or summat. Smoke blew across, so as I didn't actually see aught. Robin, he ran into it, same as ever, then there were this terrible scream!"

There was a silence for a space, then the man leaned on his stave. "'Tis a funny thing, though," he said. "For I went with Sam to see what was toward, and, well—I —I turned sick, see, when they pulled him out. And I ran off, away from the fire toward to river, that's when I came upon another fire. A small one, some bundles of old rags they were, from the tannery by the smell of 'em, because that truly did finish me, and that was where all the smoke came from."

"Do you think it was deliberately set?" asked Justin.

"I didn't give it no thought until you spoke of Rob," replied the man. He shrugged his shoulders. "Happen, and yet, like as not t'were a coincidence."

Justin sighed. "There's been a sight too many coincidences for my liking, but thank you for your information. Master Benton wished me to reward those who helped him. I hope you'll allow me to do so."

The man frowned. "Well, I will and be grateful," he said. "For with Master Benton gone, I don't know what will become of the business."

"'Tis left to his ward," said Justin.

"Aye, a maid half-grown," growled the man. "'Tis ruined we'll all be—"

"Left in trust to his ward, until such time as she is married," continued Justin. "In the meantime, her guardians will look to the business."

"Then I pray they be good men and true," said the cooper with feeling.

"I think you'll agree they are," replied Justin, handing him a gold coin. "Good day to you, Master Greenway."

⚜

Chapter Eleven

The visit to the cooper gave Justin plenty to think about as he went on his way, but his next meeting didn't go so well, wasting his time. Wat Rose had plainly sobered up from his previous evening's drinking, but he was morose and not inclined to speak, until Justin suggested payment. "Aye, I'll take Miser Benton's money if you be throwing it at me," he snarled. "'Tis true, is it, he's dead?"

"Yes, it's true," agreed Justin, eyeing him distastefully as he handed over a silver coin.

"Well, what do 'ee want to know?" Wat demanded peevishly, anxious now he had the coin in his hand, to spend it.

"Did you see anything—anything, mind—unusual on the night of the Beltane fire, when Robin Tripp was killed?"

"No, I didn't see anything at all. The smoke blinded me and got into my throat. I were choking, I hadn't time to be watching cocksure fools like Robin Tripp make a show of himself."

"You didn't care for him?" Justin asked with an air of innocence.

"Care for him? A jumped-up, good-for-nothing 'prentice lad, he be. Who were he to come tell us how to jump? Him and his tumbles and twists, more like a clown than a proper jumper."

"Were you a good jumper?" asked Justin slyly.

"Aye, I jumped in the traditional manner, mind. None of this fancy footwork, trying to make it look something it weren't, like Robin Tripp."

"I imagine you had to be light on your feet, and sober to jump the fire," Justin continued innocently.

"I've jumped these past five years, since the King came again," the man snapped. "I hadn't had no complaints."

Justin shrugged. "But you noticed the smoke?"

"I've just told you, it damn near choked me," the man snapped again. "Of course I noticed the smoke, it ruined my best jump! By the time I'd finished coughing, didn't have no breath for it, and then Robin tripped

—aye, well-named he were, that day!" He laughed in a malicious way.

"He tripped?" Justin asked in surprise, disregarding this.

"Must have done," replied the baker snappishly. "His hair were all burned away and his face and shoulders one big burn. If he'd fallen in mid-jump, t'would have been his legs and nether regions."

Justin nodded as he understood his words. "Yes, yes, I see," he said slowly. "You didn't see what tripped him, I suppose, for the smoke."

"That's what I said," he snarled. "Mind, it couldn't have been anything in his path, for we always check the run up. Aye, and a lad stands by, to make sure no sticks fall in the way, too."

"A lad?" asked Justin quickly.

"Aye, t'were Widow Tidmarsh's boy. We give him a groat, and he watches for burning logs and the like."

"Where will I find young Master Tidmarsh?" asked Justin eagerly, for in his opinion, young boys made good witnesses.

"Yonder in Abbey church-yard," returned the baker sourly.

"Dead?" asked Justin, appalled.

"Aye, slipped and fell in a ditch one dark night. He were set up by those rogues in Twin Alley, I dare say," replied the man carelessly.

"Killed?" asked Justin shocked.

"Never came to himself again," he replied. "Laid in his bed over a week and never as much as moved a muscle. Then he upped and died."

"Yet another," Justin muttered, half to himself.

"If you be finished with poking your nose in, I'm for the alehouse!" announced the baker.

"No, wait!" imperiously, Justin snapped his fingers. "What thought you of Saul Makepiece?"

"Saul Makepiece? It's him you've in mind, eh?" the baker shrugged his narrow shoulders. "Aye, like as not he were behind it if t'were foul play, for Saul weren't one to fight fair and square."

"So I've heard. Was he taken with Mistress Sophia's charms, perhaps?"

"Saul? Nay!" He gave a coarse laugh. "You're out there, my friend! He'd no designs on that jade, his quarry were Robin himself. That's as like as not why he tripped him —if he did—because Robin rejected his advances."

Justin felt his head was in a whirl, he needed time to sit quietly and think. "I see, it was that way, was it?"

he said blankly. "Well, I'm obliged for your help," he hesitated, then, unable to stop himself added: "Do take that money to your poor wife, there's a good fellow."

"Give it to that scold to waste on her whinging brats, never," he cried. "I'm off to find a game to increase this tenfold."

Justin sighed as the man scurried away, and obedient to his conscience, spent the next hour and more seeking out Sally Rose, to give her some money and some advice.

❧

Justin finally returned to the Greyhound, to bespeak him some food, to call for his and Hal's account, and to have their goods transported to Master Benton's house.

"'Tis true, then?" asked Mistress Blackwell, bringing him a tankard of ale. "Is Master Benton dead?"

"Yes, 'tis true, rest his soul," Justin replied.

"Amen to that," said the woman, her face pale. "Dear God, to be taken so quick. It don't bear thinking on."

"Indeed no," agreed Justin, hastily tucking into the excellent bowl of broth set before him.

"How is everything left, I wonder?" she asked, glancing at him from the corner of her eyes.

"In trust for Mistress Sophia," he replied indistinctly through a mouthful of bread, for it was past three in the afternoon, and he was famished.

"In trust, you say?" the landlady nodded her head. "She'll be in the care of a guardian, or trustee, then?"

"Two guardians," Justin agreed.

She sighed heavily. "Seems Adam's chances get less and less," she remarked. "Oh, if only Tom hadn't drunk away everything."

"I thought it all went to pay fines in the war?" said Justin.

"Elmley Park did," she agreed with a sigh. "But if only he'd husbanded his money, he'd have been better able to employ a good man of law to get it restored to him. It was only after we found out Jonas Capel wasn't working for us—for all that he took our money—but for Nick Crabtree."

"He that sold Elmley Park to my brother-in-law, Guy Armstrong?" asked Justin.

"Aye, after he'd ruined it, mind. Well, the war did most of that, of course. They used to run five hundred sheep on that hill, you know, and grow wheat and barley, not to mention apples and plums, all sent to Lechlade for sale in London afore the Roundheads came and took it all. No, Nick Crabtree just continued the downward slide. It was him as sold off the Hundred Acre Wood for felling, aye, and never spent a penny to bring it about! 'Tis that what rankles with Adam. He loved that place!"

"How old was he when they lost it?" asked Justin, his sympathy stirred.

"He were eleven or twelve," she replied. "Tom came to me and said he'd have to sell, and would I be prepared to make over the lease on this place to him. He'd been ruined for his King he said, so he'd sell ale, like an honest man," she sighed. "Well, he were a comely fellow, like Adam, only with a better, cheerier manner, and I'd always a soft spot for him. I could see he'd drink the place dry in a sennight, so I said I'd only sign over the lease as a marriage portion," she smiled faintly. "I think my boldness amused him, for he agreed straight off with no questions, and he and the lad moved in here. People talked, but then they always do. I'd only been widowed six months, like, and Sam, well he were more than twenty years older. I'll not deny I was happier with Tom. He could charm the birds from the trees, I reckon—rather like Sir Henry, but he weren't steady like him. No, the drink got him, like I said it would, only I managed to keep him going for ten years or so, until Adam were growed, anyway."

"I'm certain you did your best, Mistress Blackwell."

"Aye," she agreed. "But I could never get it out of either of 'em's head. It was always 'when we return to Elmley Park' or 'if we get the Park back again, we could'," she sighed again. "Such a waste of time, crying for the moon."

"But a very common human failing," Justin agreed.

"I doubt a clever gentleman like you ever did such a thing," she said smiling.

"I went one better," he replied. "I whistled down the wind a fortune, to wed my true love."

"What? Do you regret it?" she cried, shocked.

"In my saner moments, I regret the money," he replied, "but never my Bess."

She smiled. "We shall miss you when you've gone, you and Sir Henry."

"I don't think your stepson would agree," Justin said with a laugh.

"Ah, but you're wrong," she replied. "He said only this morning how it brought credit to the house for Sir Henry to stay here. I don't know what Sir Henry said to Adam, but he seems to have mended his speech, for which I am most grateful. Why, his father would have been turning in his grave to hear him talk before. Ah, here is Sir Henry, finished with those lawyers. My, but he looks so fine accompanied by the Mayor and Aldermen. I must away to attend to their dinner, they all dine here when the Sessions are finished, you know."

Justin continued with his meal as she bustled away, but stopped short as Hal looked in.

"Mistress Blackwell said you were in here, come join us at dinner. I don't see why I should be bored by all these worthy gentlemen alone."

Justin grinned. "You do look stern in that wig," he remarked. "I vow my knees would knock if I were in the dock awaiting sentence."

Hal snatched if off and flicked it at him. "I'm away to change from these, do you go into the parlour."

"Wait, Hal, all our bags are gone," said Justin. "I had them sent to Master Benton's house."

Hal goggled at him. "Master Benton's house? Are you mad?" he cried. "We can't stay there."

"Someone must, Sophie can't be left alone," Justin replied, a little taken aback by his response.

"Neither can we go there!" Hal cried, pale faced. "It will look—odd!"

"Her guardians coming to her aid? It would look odder if we didn't," said Justin puzzled. "Don't fret, I've sent word to your sister Mary explaining we needed a chaperone. I expect her, or Cecily, or both, to be there by now."

"Mary!" he cried, by no means pleased. "I'm surprised she can spare the time."

"I didn't say she'd be happy," grinned Justin. "Just there."

"But Justin, I must travel to Chipping Barbury tomorrow, I've a case to hear there. I planned to be home by Wednesday evening!"

"I, too," he agreed ruefully. "But unpleasant though it is, we were named Sophie's guardians."

"I never agreed to it!" snapped Hal.

"So you've said," agreed Justin wearily. "Repeatedly. But do you, in all honesty, intend to abandon the child?"

Hal tore off his robe impatiently, casting it aside. "No, I suppose not," he muttered, sounding almost sulky.

"Then it stands to reason we must resign ourselves to a further stay here," said Justin reasonably. "We must see Master Benton buried, and make some arrangements for Mistress Sophia at the very least, before we can think of leaving."

Hal stood silent, gazing from the window onto the busy yard, wandering how he was going to manage to live in the same house as Sophie. Then, he shrugged his shoulders. "If there's no help for it," he said, "there's no help for it. I must go and put on my coat. Do go and talk to the Mayor and Town Council for me, Justin, you are better at that sort of thing than I."

Chapter Twelve

"Psst! Sophie!" Adam Blackwell came along the garden path to where she sat sadly in her shady bower. "Alice let me in to see you. Dearest, I am so sorry for your loss. I know how fond you were of your guardian."

She smiled up at him, her eyes swimming with tears. "Dear Adam, how kind of you to take trouble to come and see me. Yes, I am a little moped, you know, I suppose it is only natural, but he was the last link with the past. Now everyone is gone and I am so alone."

He nodded sympathetically, pressing a posy of wild flowers into her hand. "I picked these for you, I know you like them," he said shyly.

"Oh Adam, thank you." She reached up on tiptoe to kiss his tanned face. "You are such a darling."

"Am I?" he replied, a ready colour staining his cheeks. "Really, Sophie?"

"Yes, Adam, but I don't mean anything by it, you know," she replied, her face suddenly troubled. "I am fond of you. I think you are an excellent fellow, but I don't love you."

"I don't care for that, Sophie," he said humbly. "If you'll only let me love you, I have enough love for both of us."

"You are such a good man, Adam," she replied, patting his hand which was clasping hers. "I am proud of you, now you've learnt to mind you speech again, and have taken on the manners of a gentleman. It matters not if you serve ale, so long as you speak fair to all men."

"Yes, I realise that," he said. "That's why I've tried so hard. I know this isn't the time or place, Sophie, but you know how much I love you, if you'll but say you'll marry me, I'll settle everything for you. I swear to you you'll never have another day's worry in your life."

"Oh, Adam!" she pulled away her hand impatiently. "I've just told you I don't love you. Can't you let it rest at that? Can't we just be friends?"

"Friends?" he asked incredulously. "Friends, but I love you, Sophie."

"Yes, I know you do, Adam," she replied more gently.

"But I—"

"Don't love me—yes I know," he snapped. "What I am saying is, you could love me, in time."

She shook her head. "No," she said, with a gentleness that was somehow convincing.

"I'm sure you could if you tried, Sophie," he cried desperately.

"But I don't want to try, Adam," she said it as kindly as possible. "It's not that I wouldn't, more that I can't. I love another."

"Another!" he cried, his cheeks suddenly pale. "Who?"

"I don't want to talk of it, Adam," she replied, and it was her turn to blush now, her eyes shining suddenly as she thought of her love. "I know it is hopeless, but I can't help myself. I am a little like you, I just love him anyway."

"Why is it hopeless? Is it that fop, Durward? I don't know what you see in him, Sophie!"

"No, it's not him," she cried indignantly. "Why he couldn't hold a candle to—but never mind that. I only told you so you'd understand."

"What is there to understand?" he cried. "You love another who doesn't return your regard—"

"I didn't say that," she cried. "He loves me." She

caught herself up. "I don't want to talk of it," she repeated.

"Well, do you imagine I do?" he cried angrily. "It's hardly a source of joy to me to hear of your infatuation for another."

"Why do you call it that?" she asked, anger putting an edge to her voice. "You say you love me and I do you the courtesy of believing you. Yet you seek to belittle my feelings?"

"I beg your pardon, ma'am, I'm sure!" he snapped, feeling hurt.

"Your petulance is neither charming, nor well bred," Sophie replied tartly. "If you've nothing more to say, I suggest you leave."

"I'm going!" he snarled, getting to his feet, intolerably hurt. "I know when I am not wanted! You think you are so clever, Sophie, so awake to all that is going on, but you'll see. You'll be glad to marry me at the last!"

"Over my dead body!" she cried, as he stalked away in a fury.

"What? More dead bodies?" asked Ned, coming from the house with Cecily, as Adam brushed past with a curt apology. "Good afternoon, Mistress Redcroft, do recollect me? I'm Ned Westwood, I've accompanied

Mistress Armstrong and my betrothed Mistress Cecily, here. They've come to keep you company."

"Mistress Armstrong?" she cried. "Oh, to keep me company, but why?"

"You'd not want to be here alone with Sir Henry and Mr Danvers for company, would you?" asked Cecily smiling. "So Mary and I have come to rest for a few days from our house cleaning. I hope we don't intrude, but we thought you'd be more comfortable with some women in the house."

"Oh, thank you, how kind. But Mistress Armstrong is so busy, I am ashamed to put her to so much trouble."

"I assure you it's no trouble," said Ned. "Mary said she was looking forward to the rest, and the chance to see what was in the shops. Come, she's in the parlour, unpacking her sewing."

Hal yawned cavernously. "God, I don't know why dining with so many worthy men should be so exhausting, but it is."

"Mmn," said Justin, joining him in a yawn, as they walked up the silent High Street, side by side in the moonlight. "So, what do you make of everything I've told you, Hal?"

"Nothing, I'm too weary," he returned, unconsciously slowing his steps as Master Benton's handsome house came into view. "I'll think about it on my ride to Chipping Barbury tomorrow."

"And you'll return here in the evening?" asked Justin anxiously.

"I suppose I must," he agreed with great reluctance. "Although I really ought to go and explain to Libby."

"I've already written explaining to both her and Bess," said Justin, halting before the door and pulling sharply on the bell.

The door flew open at once, before Hal had time to reply, to disclose Sophie's pale face. "Oh, you've come at last!" she cried. "I'd begun to despair of you. You've been an age!"

"We've been guests of the Mayor at supper," said Justin. "Is Mary come?"

"Yes, Mistress Armstrong and Mistress Cecily are both come—with Ned Westwood as escort," she said quickly. "Mistress Armstrong said not to wait supper upon you, so we didn't, but would you care for some broth? I can fetch a bowl immediately. Are you cold? The night has turned chill—shall I call for the servant to set a fire?"

"No, no, we shall do very well thank you," said Justin smiling. "For myself, I couldn't eat another thing. The Mayor and his townsmen see themselves very well. But Hal hardly ate a thing, he might yet be ahungered."

"You didn't eat?" cried Sophie anxiously. "Are you sick? Do you still have the headache? Shall I fetch you another tisane?"

"No, no, I shall do very well, I am sure my headache will go once I sleep, but thank you for your care," replied Hal, rather stiffly.

"Well, do you come on up to the parlour then, Hal," said Mary, leaning over the handsome carved staircase, her lovely face smiling in the candlelight. "And don't keep poor Sophie talking in the hall."

"Mary," Hal ran up the staircase quickly and embraced her. "My dear, I'm sorry to call upon you in this infamous fashion."

"Pooh, nonsense," she replied, kissing him soundly. "I was glad to come, both I and Cecily—and Ned too, I dare say. I told Guy to rid us of that pestilent fellow before we return."

"Which is a pity, because he'll take Jasper too, and he's a grand fellow," said Ned, as they entered the parlour arm in arm. "Cecily thinks so, don't you?"

"Yes," she agreed, coming to hug Hal and Justin, whilst Sophie, who'd followed in their wake, frowned. "Yes, I like him much more, now I know him. Are you ill, Hal?" she paused, scanning his pale face.

"My dear, I've sat all day in a stuffy courtroom listening to lawyers—and all evening in a parlour listening to merchants—my head aches," Hal laughed. "A good night's sleep followed by a ride in the fresh air will cure me of my megrims."

"Oh, I would that I could go with you!" Sophie cried. "A ride to Chipping Barbury is just what I need, too, Mistress Armstrong, could we not all go?"

"My dear," Mary looked shocked. "Go on a pleasure outing, when your guardian is barely cold and still lies unburied? What would your neighbours say?"

"Fusty old fidgets!" cried Sophie, taken aback by this view and suddenly embarrassed by her words, she decided to brazen it out. "What can they matter?"

"Public opinion always matters," said Hal sharply. "Whilst we have to live in the world—and we all do —few of us can afford to offend our neighbours. Heiress, or no."

Sophie's eyes filled with tears. "I did not mean to offend," she cried in distress. "I just so wanted to—" She turned away to hide her face, hunting in her sleeve for her handkerchief.

"Hal, do you have to be so brutal?" cried Mary, her ready sympathy stirred. "Poor Sophie's had a bad shock today."

"Then I'm surprised she's still from her bed," he snapped. "She'd be much better in it, sleeping! And shock or no, if we must take on the position of her guardians, she'd better hear the truth from our lips than offend public opinion from ignorance."

"I'm sure if you don't want to be my guardian, you'll be able to find a way out of such an arduous chore?" snapped Sophie, tears running down her nose.

"Unfortunately, there is no choice," replied Hal harshly. "Justin's opinion is we must honour Master Benton's wishes, and after consideration, I fear he is correct."

"Well, I'm sorry it is so distasteful to you," Sophie retorted, stung by the words.

"Yes," said Hal coldly. "I'm sorry, too."

"Hal!" said Mary, as Ned and Cecily looked amazed at his harshness.

"In fact, as your guardian—and I'm sure Justin agrees with me in this—you'd better go to bed. Hal continued in the same relentless fashion. "I don't know what Mary is about, to let you stay up so late, when you are plainly hysterical. Tomorrow, when you are calmer, Mary and Cecily will help you arrange some suitable mourning clothes." Then, as Sophie began to protest, he added: "No, no more. Perhaps, Cecily, you can see Sophie to her chamber?"

"I don't need an escort to bed!" cried Sophie angrily. "I am not a child!"

"Your behaviour belies your assertion," he replied. "And I will not tolerate tantrums. Now go!"

"That was a bit harsh, Hal," said Justin, as Sophie fled from the parlour, followed by Cecily, and, after she'd delivered a few pithy words, Mary.

"Justin, it has been a long day," Hal replied wearily. "One of alarums and excursions followed by tedium beyond compare, and I'd had a headache as a companion to it the whole time. I do not need the hysteria of a spoilt child at its close, or a lecture from you in how to comport myself. Now, if you'll excuse me, plainly I am at odds with the rest of the world, and would probably benefit from a period of solitude. I'll bid you both good night."

Ned blew out his cheeks as the door closed after Hal. "Phew, he's in a pucker, what's amiss? Is he ill?"

"I don't know," said Justin frowning. "I don't think so—well, nothing physical, anyway."

Ned frowned as he poured him a goblet of wine. "What do you mean?" he asked.

"I mean nothing ails him bodily. It's in his head," Justin stood frowning, too.

"You think the headache is serious?" asked Ned, a shade of anxiety entering his tone. "They say that it's the headache at the start of the plague, and he's been shut up in that courtroom with all manner of rogues and such! All alive with heaven knows what awful sicknesses. You know the reports from London are getting really bad with many people dying of the plague. There's even a rumour that the Court may leave London!"

"It is so every year," said Justin dismissively. "They said so this time last year, but not that many people died. No, you mistake my meaning. I mean he is troubled in his mind by something."

"He has been ever since my father died last year in France," agreed Ned.

"Yes, it might just be that they'd not truly made up their quarrel," said Justin. "But I've a feeling this is something new, more recent."

"A case that has worried him, perhaps?" suggested Ned.

"Yes, perhaps," Justin agreed, although he didn't really think so. "Either way, like Hal, I'm for my bed. It's been a long, difficult day, and I foresee another tomorrow." He glanced to the younger man. "You can come with me, if you want. I don't suppose you speak French like Hal, do you?"

"None but the French speak French like Hal," said Ned gloomily. "I don't hold with foreigners."

"Yes, I prefer them in their own country," replied Justin as they snuffed the candles. "But I'd not mind Hal's fluency tomorrow, whilst dealing with Dr Douay."

Hal's precipitate withdrawal did not ensure a sound night's sleep, and dawn found him still weary and jaded in spirits, as he made ready for his journey to the next town to hear the trial of an elderly woman accused of infanticide. The mere thought of it depressed him, for he'd seen the depositions, which hinted at all manner of dark practices, including witchcraft, and he shrank from the tortuous hours listening to one side, or the other. He wasn't one to shirk duty, however, so he shrugged himself into his coat, picked up his hat and gloves, and opened his door softly, so as not to disturb others sleeping nearby.

Not softly enough, though, to allow Sophie to continue with her slumbers. She started up from the window seat in the hall, where she'd been curled half the night, clutching a cover about her.

"Oh, Hal, is it morning?" she cried, then as he shushed her severely, she smiled at him. "I'm sorry," she whispered. "But I was frightened I might miss you."

"How long have you been here?" he asked, keeping his voice low.

"Not long," she lied. "But I wanted to see you before you went, to say goodbye."

"I shall be back this evening, for Heaven's sake," he snapped crossly, for once again his heart was leaping like a mad thing at the sight of her.

"Will you?" She clasped his sleeve, and gazed up at him adoringly.

"I've told you," he replied roughly. "I have no choice."

"Why are you so unkind to me?" she asked reproachfully. "I've done nothing to anger you."

"Just by being, you anger me," he cried, anger leaping into his voice. "Don't you see? Won't you understand? This cannot go on!"

She gazed up at him mutely, tears welling into her

eyes at his roughness, so that his heart smote him, and before he knew what he was doing, he'd pulled her into his arms and was kissing her face, her eyes, her lips. "Oh dear God, forgive me!" he muttered. "I love you, I love you, now go, go and leave me my sanity!"

He thrust her from him, and clattered down the stairs as if pursued by all the devils from Hell, whilst Sophie stood, her cover clasped about her, her eyes shining, tears of joy coursing down her cheeks. She continued so for another few moments, lingering over the encounter, reliving it, then she turned away slowly, and walked back along the dim corridor to her own chamber, so deep in her dreams as to not notice the silent closing of Justin's door.

⚜

"Well I, for one, don't believe it!" Ned declared later that morning, his jaw setting stubbornly, as they made their way through the bustle of the streets.

"Believe me, I do not want to," Justin replied as they walked down the High Street towards the Sign of the Golden Key. "I am as fond of Hal as you are, and Libby is my sister. This is the worst mess in the world to me."

"And he actually said he loved her?" Ned was incredulous.

"Yes," said Justin, looking haggard.

"Well, I thought he quite disliked her," said Ned frowning. "I mean, I've never seen him give her more than a few odd words, and last night he tore into her, and sent her to bed like a child."

"Yes, like the child he would prefer her to be," Justin agreed.

"And he's devoted to Libby and the children," continued Ned. "No, you've made a mistake, Justin, most like you dreamed it. You said you awoke with a start. You probably confused everything in your dream."

"I awoke at Hal's voice raised in anger," he replied. "I may have been startled, but not stupid. I heard and saw."

"Well, I don't know," said Ned stiffly. "Perhaps you did, but you need have no fear, my brother is a gentleman. He'll not allow his wife or children to suffer."

"I know Hal to be an honourable man," snapped Justin. "I have no doubts as to his integrity. Neither Libby nor the children will suffer, but Hal will, and so shall Sophie. As her guardian, she must be my main concern."

Ned nodded. "Aye, I take your point, she must be married, and as quickly as possible."

"At last we are in agreement," cried Justin, halting outside the house. "Excellent, then you'll help me promote the idea, and Adam Blackwell's suit."

"If you think it will help Hal," Ned replied doubtfully.

"It's the only answer, poor devil, no wonder he wanted to leave Chawcester and never come back! Listen, we must get little Cecily to help, she'll be invaluable in persuading Sophie that Adam Blackwell is a good match. Right, here's the place. Dear God, I do wish Hal were here to help with this."

They entered the darkened shop and inhaled the strong scents, the mere smell of which made Ned think of Aunt Margery's stillroom and all the unpleasant brews she kept there. The ceiling was festooned with all manner of herbs, some of which brushed the top of Ned's head as he went forward, making him shudder.

A small, dark-haired man with mobile features and a moustache came from before the fire, where he had been stirring a blackened cauldron. "Good day to you gentlemen, do I find you well?"

"Tolerable well, thank you," said Justin, surprised. "I'm looking for Monsieur Douay, the French physician."

"And you have found him," he replied, with scarcely a trace of accent. "How may I assist you?"

"You don't sound like a Frenchy," said Ned bluntly.

"Ah, you want I should assume ze 'eavy accent, you feel my cure will be more efficacious?" he replied, his eyes twinkling.

"No, not at all," replied Justin grinning. "We were just expecting…"

"The wizened ancient? The magician with the foreign tongue? Well, sometimes for the commonfolk and good wives of the town it is so, but you gentlemen surely do not need such subterfuge? How are you troubled?"

"We aren't ill," said Ned quickly.

"We are troubled by the death of Edmund Benton," said Justin. "The apothecary tells me you prescribed a sovereign remedy for him last spring."

"Yes," agreed the man, indicating that they should sit at a gate-leg table covered in books, some of which bore strange symbols. He moved aside a flask and a few bowls containing muddy-looking concoctions, and Ned gingerly took a seat on a stool. "I did so in May, after he'd had some unpleasant effects of his increasing age. I also told him he must take life more slowly, which he promised to do but then his young assistant was killed, and I knew that he would not be long in following. It is often the way."

"I think he was poisoned," said Justin bluntly.

The man's eyebrows rose in surprise. "I heard nothing of this from Master Cresswell."

"No, unfortunately Master Cresswell thinks I am accusing him of an ill-prepared remedy, which I am not," said Justin. "I would be obliged if you would examine Master Benton for me, Dr Douay, and give me your opinion."

"What is it you think he took?" the doctor frowned.

"I think he was given something, I'm not sure what. Perhaps you can help, it would appear he arrived home from a visit—and a long ride—feeling ill. He had aches in his limbs, and stumbled on getting from his horse. He then went to bed, refusing to send for either you or the apothecary, and it seems he never moved again."

The physician made a face. "Many poisons could be indicated by such a history. I will view the corpse myself."

"Thank you sir, that is exactly as I wished," said Justin. "Will you come with us now?"

"Indeed, I will," he replied. "This sounds most interesting." He gathered up a hat and cloak and following them from the shop, and back the way they had come. No more did his mind alter after he'd made a full examination of the body in the company of Justin, for Ned had suddenly recollected that he needed to spend some time with Cecily.

"Yes," the physician repeated. "Most interesting, Mr Danvers. I do believe you to be correct. It is quite likely Master Benton was poisoned. See how he is so very stiff in his pose, even though the rigour has now passed away, and here, if you look in his mouth, his tongue bitten through. Only great pain will cause a man to do so."

"Yet he did not cry out or move," said Justin. "I saw him first thing yesterday morning and he lay in bed, as if sleeping, with barely a cover disturbed."

"Oui," nodded the Doctor. "Yes, this confirms it. He did not move, because he could not move, the poison paralysed his limbs slowly. You said, I think, he complained of pain in his legs?"

"And stumbled on getting from his horse. He had to be helped to bed," said Justin. "What do you think killed him?"

"Several poisons are indicated," he replied. "Of which, hemlock is perhaps the most common—or of course, it could just have been a heart attack, so sudden he was too weak with pain to cry out or move."

"But surely if it were a heart attack, would he not have blue nails?" asked Justin quickly. "Possibly, yes, probably," agreed the physician, nodding. "But physicking is not a definite science, Mr Danvers, I could not swear to any of it."

"But in your opinion?" persisted Justin.

The Frenchman stood gazing at the corpse, arrayed in his funeral clothes. "I'd say he met his end at the hand of another," he agreed.

⚜

Chapter Thirteen

"Oh Hal, I am so glad you are finally come!" Sophie opened the heavy front door to him and fell upon his neck again.

"Dear God, child, I told you I'd return!" he cried irritably, loosening her hands. "Do try for a little conduct! Your behaviour grows more hoydenish daily."

"Wat Rose is dead!" she cried, falling away, tears springing to her eyes.

"Wat Rose, the baker?' he replied in astonishment, his ill-temper arrested.

"Yes, Sally came weeping to the door, not an hour since. He was found drowned in a barrel of ale!"

"A fitting end," sighed Hal. "Inevitable, I expect, the man was a drunkard."

"Justin has gone with her, taking Dr Douay and Ned to see the corpse," she cried. "He seemed to think it was another murder. Sally thinks so too!"

Hal took off his cloak wearily. It had been a very hard day, and the litigation every bit as lengthy and tedious as he'd dreaded. His judgement had met with little approbation from the authorities in Chipping Barbury, and although he was sure in his mind of his principles, in his imagination, he'd been looking forward to discussing the case with Justin over a quiet supper, free of alarms and aggravation.

"I fail to see why he should jump to that conclusion," he snapped. "Is every inebriate to be considered as a murder victim now? Shall I be obliged to lock up all ale drapers?"

"It's on account of Uncle Edmund, I think," she said, rather pale-faced now, for in his irritation he was cold and aloof, and she feared his mood. "Monsieur Douay came at noon with Justin and Ned and examined Uncle Edmund's body. He says he is certain Uncle Edmund was poisoned." Tears began to fall down her cheeks. "The physician examined Uncle Edmund's mouth, it seems, and found he'd bitten through his tongue." Her lips trembled over the words. "Poor Uncle Edmund, to die in such pain, and alone!"

Mechanically, he took her into his arms to comfort

her. "Shush, shush, don't weep," he soothed gently. "You weren't to know. Did the French physician say what had killed him?"

She shook her head, burying her face in his coat, inhaling the mingled scents, which were him, taking much comfort from his closeness. "He said he couldn't be sure in his mind, that it could be any one of several poisons, but that from the symptoms I described, he thought it may possibly be hemlock."

"Hemlock?" Hal repeated in surprise. "That is no accident then. Hemlock must mean murder."

"So Justin said," she agreed. "He spent the afternoon writing out the case, he said, so that you and he could go through it together tonight. But that was before Sally came weeping at the door. He then hurried off with Ned, saying you were to follow when you arrived."

Hal stiffened, realised he'd been cuddling her, and put her firmly from him. "I'll do so in my own good time, if at all," he said tartly. "I've been the whole day at the beck and call of justice. I'll not spend the evening at Justin's beck and call as well."

"No, well, besides which, I thought when he'd gone, 'twas likely you'd want to be with your wife, anyway," Sophie said slowly.

"Indeed," he said, with undue emphasis. "If it were possible, but as we've said, we must remain here."

"Yes, but she is come," said Sophie, glancing up at him, her face troubled. "Lady Westwood is here!"

"Libby? Here?" he cried in amazement. "No, she cannot be, not here!"

"She arrived this afternoon," replied Sophie, her eyes never leaving his face. "She said she'd come to relieve Mistress Armstrong, whom she knew to be busy, and that if I had been left to you and her brother's guardianship, she was the chiefest person to look after me." She observed the consternation on his face and added: "I told her I was sorry to be such a trouble to her."

"My God!" he cried angrily. "This must be Justin's doing. If she has taken any harm—"

"Mistress Armstrong was most concerned too," agreed Sophie. "She insisted Lady Westwood went straight to bed, for I must confess she was uncommonly pale and very weary—"

"Dear God!" he groaned. "Where is she now? Is she ill? Did she bring the children with her?"

"She's abed," said Sophie, as he mounted the stairs two at a time. "Cecily is sitting with her. She came alone, apart from her manservant. She told Mistress

Armstrong she'd left the children in Jane's and Bess's care, but that she might send for the baby, if your stay was going to be protracted," Sophie sighed as she hurried after him. "Mistress Armstrong said not to disturb her."

"Damn Mary," he snapped, mounting the second flight of stairs. "She should have sent for me immediately."

"Lady Westwood wouldn't allow it. She said you'd be home soon enough and only went to bed on the condition that Mistress Armstrong returned to her home. That's when Cecily and Ned decided to stay here. I put Lady Westwood in your chamber."

Hal barely heard the last of this, but the sense of her words penetrated as he opened the door into his chamber.

Cecily sat at the foot of the bed in a room lit by a single candle. She looked up and smiled reassuringly at him. "She's asleep, Hal," she hissed. "And has been this past hour or more."

"Thank God for that," he said devoutly. "Why, in heaven's name, did she come? Why take such a risk, when she's only just recovered from the birth of baby Francis?"

"She said she was worried for your health," said Cecily, as he moved to the head of the bed, looking down on the sleeping figure anxiously. His eyes scanned the pallid face of his wife laid out on the white pillows. She was so pale that fear clutched at him again. "When Justin wrote to say you'd be delayed, she decided that you needed her company," continued Cecily.

"I need her health more than her company," Hal replied, leaning over to stroke the tumbled hair from Libby's damp brow, whilst Sophie, who had gained the room, stood in the doorway, mesmerised.

"Hal, is that you?" Libby stirred, her hand coming out to clasp his. "Hal, are you come at last?"

"I am here," he caught her hand firmly and covered it with his other, kneeling beside her. "My dear, what are you doing here? Why have you taken such a risk with your health?"

"Justin said you needed me," she said, her voice a sigh. "I've missed you so much, Hal. Nothing is the same since you went away. It's like the sun being hidden by cloud."

"My dear," he said quietly. "I told you I'd be home as soon as I may. You need not have fretted for me. I pray you've not done yourself an injury by this day's work."

She smiled at him, shaking her head. "Mostly, I am weary," she said in a threadlike voice. "Better tomorrow. Kiss me, Hal, and tell me that you love me, then I'll sleep sounder."

"You know how I love you," he said, bending over her and feeling like Judas. He kissed her damp brow, and then as she moved her head, her cheek, and finally her lips. "Sleep Libby, we'll talk again tomorrow," he murmured, as Sophie, with an inarticulate noise, scampered away. He waited whilst Libby closed her eyes, and then glancing to Cecily, hissed: "Have you eaten supper?"

"Yes, Sophie sat with her earlier whilst I ate. Do you go down and get some supper, it's all laid out for you," replied Cecily. "I shall do very well here."

"Thank you Cecily, I'm obliged to you," he said, sliding from the bed and making for the door with an air of determination.

He found Sophie, red-eyed but contained, at the supper table, which was laid out with almost a festive air. "Were you expecting company?" he asked, glancing about.

"Only you, Justin and Ned," she whispered.

"Then such display is not seemly, with your guardian still above ground," he said severely.

Tears stung her lids at his harshness, but she ignored them, instead, putting a question of her own. "My neighbours are asking for news of the funeral. What should I say?"

"That it can go forward immediately, once the town bailiff has seen Master Benton's corpse and listened to Dr Douay," Hal replied curtly. "Tomorrow afternoon would be advisable. Send word to all his acquaintances, and set your woman to preparing food. That should give you something to occupy your time."

"I do not need something to occupy my time," she cried, tears trickling down her face. "Why do you speak so to me? What have I done that you must treat me so ill? It is not my fault that your wife is come."

"No, but it's your fault I feel so damned guilty when I look at her!" he snapped unpardonably. "If I'd never met you, I'd not be in this intolerable position."

"What position?" she replied, stung. "I don't see that you are in any position. It is I who suffer, I who love you to desperation. You don't care about me at all."

"I would to God that were true," he said, and there was great bitterness in his voice.

"It is not then?" she cried. "You've just told your wife you love her, yet if you love her, you can't love me, and yet you told me this morning that you loved me."

"Don't be so foolish! Don't you see, I have no right to love you," he replied angrily. "My duty is to my wife and I love her dearly."

"So you lied to me this morning," she wept.

"Yes! No! Oh! God help me! Look, I've told you I am a married man, I cannot love you. Now let that be an end to it!"

She laid her golden head on the table and wept with heartrending sobs. "Oh, how can it be an end to it?" she whispered. "Just because you say it must be, it doesn't mean it will be. I still love you, whatever you say to me or do, I will always love you!"

"This is intolerable," he repeated, his teeth gritted.

"What shall I do?" she asked. "How can I live? Where shall I go?"

"Listen to me, Sophie, and listen well," he said sternly, his face pale. "You say you love me, if that is so, then you must learn to comport yourself properly, or I shall be forced to explain the situation to my brother-in-law, and leave at once. I will not tolerate this kind of behaviour on each occasion we meet. To continue in this manner will send us both mad. The feelings we have must, and shall, be contained and controlled, or

I shall have no alternative but to remove myself from your presence, and never see you again."

"What feelings do you have?" she demanded. "You talk of control and containment, but you don't say what you feel, except guilt. Why do you feel guilt?"

"Because I have betrayed my wife," he replied coldly. "I swore to love her, forsaking all other, so long as we both shall live," he ended, quoting from the Book of Common Prayer.

"And you no longer do?" she asked, turning her tearstained face upon him.

"I still love her dearly," he replied, his tone unsteady. "But I cannot, at this moment in time, forsake you."

"Then you do love me!" she said quickly. "Tell me so!"

"What difference does it make if I do say I love you," he cried in exasperation, "except that it makes it more real, more difficult to forget."

"Because it makes it more real," she cried. "Because I need to know!"

"Have done!" Hal said sharply, a warning in his voice, which his family would have recognised.

"Tell me!" she commanded, unaware she was playing with fire.

Hal brought his hand down flat on the table, making the dishes jump. "I said: have done!" he said in a voice of thunder.

"Sophie, has none ever told you: never tease a hungry man over supper?" said Justin, as he entered. He took in the scene at a glance, continuing smoothly: "I was hoping you'd join me, Hal, to view Wat Rose's body, but you plainly have other plans for this evening."

"I have no plans, other than requiring supper," Hal snapped. "Not an unreasonable request, surely, after a long day and twenty mile round journey."

"Send for your servants, Sophie," commanded Justin, as Ned, having spoken to Cecily, came to join them. "Tomorrow, I'll get my sister to explain to you the wisdom of not enacting a farce on a man at a mealtime."

"Speaking of your sister," said Hal, as Sophie flounced from the room, "whatever possessed you to send such a message to her as to bring her here I such a rush?"

"As her legal advisor, I was looking to her best interests," replied Justin coldly.

"As her brother, were you not neglecting her health?" Hal snapped, not liking the inference.

"A fine line splits the two," Justin replied, as the servants returned, laden down with dishes of hot food. He discovered he was suddenly very hungry. "Libby's health gives me cause for concern, but ultimately, I knew she'd be in greater danger of she hadn't come."

Hal, who was inordinately hungry too, felt he'd like to challenge this, but fearful of further enlightenment, took refuge in remarking: "I suppose you imagine you know what you are talking about. But tell me, is it so, does Douay definitely think Master Benton was poisoned?"

"Yes, when he examined the body he said that Sophie's evidence, coupled with our own, makes him sure his death was not accidental. He also, at my request, came to look at Wat Rose." Justin's shrewd eyes examined Hal's ravaged countenance grimly. "He discovered a large lump on the back of the drowned man's skull, which he says, was probably administered by a club of some sort."

"A lump on his head? You mean he was hit on the head?" asked Hal blankly.

"And then thrust, unconscious, into a barrel of ale," agreed Justin.

"How do you know he was hit?" asked Hal, beginning to sip at the bowl of steaming broth set before him. "Perhaps he hit his head, and then fell into the barrel of ale? Where was this, by the way?"

"In the cellar at the Greyhound," said Justin, taking up his own spoon.

"The Greyhound?" echoed Hal. He sat for a few moments staring before him, then he said: "Either way, I can't see a manner in which a man may hit his head, and then fall into an ale barrel."

"Quite," said Justin. "Especially not headfirst into a barrel. He was upended, you know, that's how Adam Blackwell found him, his feet in the air, ale slopped everywhere."

"Aye," said Ned, finishing his broth and selecting a hunk of bread and some slices of beef. "The landlord seemed mighty put out by the waste of ale, and the mess."

"He would be," remarked Hal. "I doubt he had much sympathy for Wat Rose alive, let alone finding him dead in his cellar."

"Mmmn," said Justin. "We'll have to discover just what Adam Blackwell was doing yesterday. I don't think he's implicated, but we must explore every avenue. He claims he was out walking on the Abbey fields, looking for wild flowers to make a posy for Sophie, but can't remember meeting anyone whilst doing so."

"I imagine anybody who met such a fellow gathering flowers would well remember it," said Ned thoughtfully, helping himself to a dish of stewed fish.

"Sophie says you've written everything down, Justin," said Hal, crumbling a piece of bread onto his bowl of broth. "May I read it later? It should help to clarify matters."

"Yes," said Justin. "Do you want me to carve some of this beef for you?"

"No, I thank you," replied Hal, taking another mouthful of broth.

"I thought you were hungry," said Justin, watching him narrowly.

"So I am," Hal replied, meeting his eyes. "I am eating this excellent broth."

Ned glanced up, sensing tension between them. "The fish stew is good," he offered.

"Do you think this affair of Wat Rose bears any relation to Edmund Benton's poisoning?" asked Hal. "As I see it, he could have been the target of any of his unfortunate confederates at any time. He was a thoroughly unpleasant fellow by all accounts."

"Yes," agreed Justin with a sigh. "That's what makes it so very difficult. However, I am pretty certain in my mind that it is all connected."

"I don't think so," said Hal obstinately. "I believe you are fitting the facts to a convenient theory."

Justin stiffened. "I am aware you are anxious to be gone from this town, but I really don't think closing your eyes to what is staring you in the face will help in any way."

There was an abrupt silence at this, and it was left to Ned to say prosaically: "Well, we must remain until poor old man Benton is underground, anyway, so I don't see what you are both quarrelling about, you've until Thursday at least to decide upon the matter."

"Yes," Justin nodded. "As usual, your common sense, Ned, is most trustworthy. Things will be so much clearer by Thursday. In the meantime, Hal, I suggest we go through these papers, and see if we can make some sense of them."

"That will take until daylight," said Ned yawning.

"Then it'll take us until daylight," said Justin. "It must be done if we are to decide what to do next."

❧

Chapter Fourteen

Hal yawned as dawn broke, and passed the closely-written sheets across the table to his brother-in-law, shielding his eyes with a hand, as he rested his head on it wearily. "I've read it through twice," he said, as if in defence. "You make a good case."

"But you are not convinced," said Justin, with a hint of anger showing.

"A lot of it is coincidence," Hal replied swiftly, picking up the quill and rubbing his cheek with the feathers. "I know it holds together, but you can't deny it could all be coincidence."

"Three deaths within three weeks, coincidence?," Justin remarked irritably.

"It does happen," said Hal loftily. "You must remember this is a larger town, not a country village."

"I live in a large town," said Justin, through gritted teeth. "I don't recall there ever being three strange deaths, within three weeks of each other."

"But there aren't," protested Hal. "Robin Tripp could have been an accident. Wat Rose probably was as a result of a drunken brawl."

Justin got to his feet with a snap, picking up his bundle of notes. "Just because you've made a damn fool of yourself over a pretty face, don't expect me to ignore the facts!" he cried icily. "I'm not turning tail and running off, leaving a murderer here just because I can't control my intemperate lust!"

"One must be a gentleman to have lust, intemperate or otherwise, not a dull-as-ditchwater clerk!" Hal snapped, his temper cracking. "Don't lecture me on feelings you don't possess!"

"You have no right to such gentlemanly feeling!" Justin's eyes glinted with fury. "You are a married man."

"I am as well aware of that fact as you are." Hal also got angrily to his feet. "Neither you, nor your sister, fail to remind me of it constantly."

"More shame to you, to need reminding," cried Justin, forgetting to show caution.

"Excuse me, I must decline to continue this discussion at this present time," Hal spat over his shoulder, as he stalked from the room.

"Yes, do run away again," called Justin after him. "Don't, for heaven's sake, face up to anything!"

He sat back down, and began to go again over his papers and charts. He worked methodically through them, testing them against Hal's words, until disturbed by the arrival of Libby dressed in a bed-gown.

"Justin," she said, entering the room slowly and coming to rest her hands on the table in front of him. "Justin, what have you and Hal been quarrelling over?"

"What, has he run to you with his complaints now?" Justin cried, incensed. "And dragged you from your bed?"

"No," she replied evenly. "But 'tis plain he is in an awful temper."

"Not an uncommon occurrence," said Justin, returning to his papers.

Libby drew out a chair and sat down heavily. "I do wish you'd not annoyed him."

"Why? He annoys me," Justin replied pettishly, "with his high and mighty ways and his tantrums."

"He has much to irk him, Justin," Libby said with a sigh.

"Do we not all, Libby?" he asked, putting down the

pen again. "Good God, do we not all have problems in our daily lives? Is Hal always to be sacrosanct? Must one be forever on tiptoes round him, lest one offends his so delicate sensibilities? I tell you, he has offended mine!"

"I must do so," she replied sadly. "How has he offended you?"

"Never you mind," he replied tartly. "And why must you tiptoe round him?"

"Because I love him, silly," she replied with a sad smile. "Much as I love you, and to see you at odds wounds me."

He leaned forward to clasp her hands, his eyes searching her pale face. "It is only a falling out of principles, such as we often have," he lied, seeing her distress, and wishing to sooth her anxiety. "Don't fret, we'll soon be back on terms again."

"Will you?" she looked up, meeting his eyes. "It seems more than the usual squabble to me."

He smiled at her nursery usage, and made haste to reassure her. "Hal is out of sorts," he said. "He's had a bad time, both here, and at Chipping Barbury. I suspect old Justice Meecham deliberately took to his bed so as not to have to deal with these cases. None of Hal's judgements were met with popular acclaim."

"Hal doesn't need popular acclaim usually," she said.

"No, but it isn't easy to make difficult judgements when one is a stranger," he said. "But if one is to remain—"

"Justin, Justin, do come, come quickly!" Sophie burst into the room, she too in night attire, her lovely hair all tumbled. "Oh, I beg pardon my lady, but Justin, quickly, my maid is just come from market, and she says Sam Hedges has been murdered!"

"Sam Hedges?" he cried in astonishment, getting to his feet. "Sam Hedges, that couldn't have been a drunken brawl!"

"No, indeed," she replied trembling. "It seems he's held in the stocks, with his tongue cut out!"

"Oh, the poor man, how very dreadful!" cried Libby turning paler.

"Libby, my papers," said Justin, hastening to the door. "Collect them up for me, if you please, I must get there before he's moved! Sophie, find Sir Henry and tell him he may come to join me."

Staying only to pick up his hat in the hall, Justin hurried off to the market place, where the stocks were set up. There, he discovered a small crowd gathered around, looking mutinous, as they muttered together. Justin elbowed his way to the front, anger in his fine eyes as he saw how the dissenter had been held hand and foot, and then brutally dismembered.

"How did he die?" he demanded of the constable, who was standing guard over the figure.

"His tongue were cut out," the man indicated the grisly evidence, nailed to the post alongside the drooping head.

"That shouldn't have killed him," said Justin. "Does he have other injuries?"

"I cannot say on account of the blood," remarked the man dispassionately. "I'm waiting for the bailiff."

"May I look?" asked Justin.

"If you ain't bothered, I'm sure I'm not," the man replied. "Just as long as you don't try to take him away."

Justin gingerly lifted the jerkin and shirt, stiff with blood which was rapidly drying, looking for evidence of a stab wound. "He doesn't appear to have been knifed," he remarked, glad to go to the rear of the stocks and examine the man's back. "It must just be blood loss, then. Oh hello, he's been hit, look here, at the base of his skull." He pointed, and the constable reluctantly left his post to give the large lump on the back of the dead man's head a cursory look.

"It bled a little," he said, "but not to the front of him."

"Quite," said Justin. "But that explains how they got him here." He glanced up, looking about him. "Isn't the market square patrolled at night?"

"The Watch make their rounds," the constable agreed cautiously.

"But this must have taken time," cried Justin. "To knock out a man, to carry him hence, set him up in the stocks, to do this unspeakable thing to him."

"'Twere on account of him being a preacher, like as not," called a voice from the crowd.

"Most likely," agreed Justin, turning to them. "But is every man who raises his voice to have his tongue ripped out in order to silence him? Such barbarous days are long past. Many of you must have fought to see such crimes were never allowed again. Aye, and your comrades lost their lives too, in order that truth and justice might prevail."

"Here comes one whose task it be to bring justice," called another from the edge of the crowd as Hal came up quickly.

"Sam Hedges," he said, his face pale. "By God, who did this to the poor fellow?"

"Somebody who wanted him kept quiet," replied Justin. "The same man as killed Master Benton and Wat

Rose, by my guess."

"You have no proof—" began Hal.

"How much proof do you want?" cried Justin, incensed. "Must all Chawcester be dead around you, before you'll see what's afoot?"

"No, but shall we try for some public order?" he snapped icily. "We hardly want to start a panic or a riot."

"Not my province," snapped Justin in reply, as the crowd began to mutter amongst themselves.

"Here comes the bailiff," said Hal in relief, seeing how the crowd's mood veered all the more each moment. "Master Keeble, well met."

"Sir Henry." The bailiff was punctilious in his observance. "So, what have we here, Sambourne?"

"An unlawful killing, Master Bailiff," replied the constable with the air of one who won't be caught out.

"A killing, are we sure of that?" asked the Bailiff doubtfully. "Is it not an ill-timed jape or jest which has gone astray?"

"A man has been hit over the head, imprisoned in the stocks, and had his tongue cut out," said Justin sharply. "Surely, even in a town which still sacrifices its young men to the fire to ensure a good harvest, that's going a little too far?"

"Sacrifice young men? I don't know what you mean, Mr Danvers," he replied stiffly, as a ripple of consternation ran through the crowd again. "Sambourne, organise a hurdle, let poor Hedges be released and carried to the coffin makers."

"You saw Wat Rose, I do believe, last evening?" asked Justin, as the bailiff stood watching, whilst this was organised by the slow-thinking constable.

"Indeed, I did sir, at Sir Henry's request," he replied. "He was drowned, you know."

"Yes, I do know," said Justin shortly. "And you looked at Master Benton's body, and listened to Monsieur Duval's testimony?"

"I did, although I don't hold with Frenchies myself," he agreed. "They'll say anything, they will, I reckon!"

"And you still feel that this death is the result of a jape gone astray?" Justin continued, disregarding the man's words.

"I am resolved to take my cue from Sir Henry," said the man with a smug air. "He being a justice like, he'll know what's what."

"I—I rather think, Keeble," said Hal reluctantly, as Justin turned incredulous eyes upon him. "That this matter might bear a little investigation."

"Oh indeed, Sir Henry, if that be your wishes," agreed the man fervently. "I am only too happy to look into the matter, Sir Henry, only I were—that is to say, in my official capacity—about to attend Master Benton's funeral this afternoon."

"Are we not all?" said Hal in a soothing manner. "However, after the funeral, I do think, Keeble, you and your constables might make a few enquiries, and perhaps report any findings to myself and Mr Danvers."

"If that is what you are wanting, Sir Henry, then I shall be pleased to assist," replied the bailiff.

"Does that satisfy you?" asked Hal, as the melancholy procession set off. He and Justin had recollected that they, too, had Master Benton's funeral to attend and took themselves back to the house for breakfast and to make ready.

"Satisfy me? No!" Justin replied. "What is there in this matter to be satisfied with? We've never got anywhere near finding out who it is. Or if the murders are all connected, or whether there are two murderers in this town."

"I cannot think there would be two such men," Hal replied thoughtfully. "Although, I can still, in spite of your anger, see the possibility of some of the deaths being accidents. I cannot think such a lovely place could harbour two evil men."

"I doubt me the beauty of a town has much bearing on the souls of its inhabitants," Justin snapped.

"But I do," countered Hal. "I firmly believe poor souls forced to exist in hovels have a greater capacity for wrong doing."

"Well, even this pretty place contains hovels, I saw them myself when I went in search of Wat Rose's poor wife," retorted Justin. "I may even have seen the killer, I don't know."

"Unless there are two, the murderer would have to be acquainted with Master Benton," said Hal, as they entered the house.

"Or Robin Tripp," agreed Justin. "These last two murders have been connected with the fire dance. Which reminds me, I must tell Will Greenway to have a care of himself."

"Will Greenway," smiled Hal. "I can't see him being taken unawares in a dark alley. Come, this afternoon, after the funeral, let us sit down again and go through your papers."

"Aye," he agreed, "with no quarrelling. By the by, did

I tell you? Mistress Blackwell just now came up to me to tell me that Adam was out picking a posy yesterday afternoon, and that Sophie certainly received one from him, containing wild flowers which grow on the Common."

"You did not, but I am not surprised," he replied with a sigh. "That fellow always does seem to have an excuse, usually one given by another. I'd be happier if a neutral townsman had seen him. Any can pick flowers."

Chapter Fifteen

Libby glanced uneasily to her husband, as he sat, making a pretence of eating the food before him. The tenseness about his firm mouth and chin told her he was far from happy in his mind, and the dark shadows beneath his sombre eyes confirmed it.

It had been so since the end of last year, when news had come through finally of the death of his father and his stepmother, along with her child. Killed in a bout of plague in a small town in Gascony, the letter had said, as had been almost one half of the inhabitants. There was no denying it had been a shock to them all. Francis Westwood had come unscathed through a bloody civil war and more plots and conspiracies than any could number. To die in a dirty little town in a far-off land had struck them all as so futile. But for Hal, estranged from his father since a bitter quarrel, it had hit hardest of all, taking, it would appear, all the joy of living from him.

That Hal was already unsettled in his mind, Libby had confided to her brother, but now, here was another problem to add to their troubles. Justin had been right to send for her, it was plain to her eyes, sharpened by the intensity of her love, that Hal was desperately trying to conceal something from her. She had a sinking feeling in the pit of her stomach, that it was love for Sophia Redcroft he was so anxious to hide.

That Sophia was infatuated by Hal, there was no doubt. Libby had seen that phenomenon too many times to miss the signs. But normally, the malady was short-lived. Total incomprehension or awareness on the part of Hal, usually meant the young lady either retreated hastily from his sphere, or equally quickly, quashed her emotions, before she became an object of ridicule.

Therefore, either Sophia Redcroft was an unusually determined, spoilt and selfish young woman, or—and Libby hesitated even mentally in thinking this—she'd received some sort of encouragement from Hal. Justin, in his letter, had been cryptic, and evasive since, in his conversation. But she knew her brother well. Loyalty to Hal would mean that he'd find it impossible to betray him. Yet, in calling Libby here, he meant her to take an active hand in all his attempts to put a stop to this affair and promote peace.

"So the funeral will be over soon, Mistress Sophia," said Justin with a kindly air. "From past experience, that is the very worst moment. Thereafter, life is difficult, but there comes a certain peace with burying one's dead."

Sophie nodded. "Yes, I recollect from when we buried Mistress Nicholls and Robin, not that I held either of them in the affection that I did Uncle Edmund—" She broke off, her voice suspended in tears, and then continued in a jumble of half-sentences, in which only the words 'totally bereft' could be made out.

"Well, yes, of course you must feel so, my dear," said Libby sympathetically. "There can be nothing worse than to find yourself suddenly alone, but you must look upon us as your family now. We are here to take care of you."

"And although this isn't the time to be talking of it," said Justin. "You'll soon be able to forget all your loneliness in your own family. Sophie, I think—and I'm sure Sir Henry agrees with me—that an early marriage is indicated for you. Of course, we'll wait for a period of mourning, but once that is over, I don't see why you shouldn't be married to Adam Blackwell immediately."

"Adam Blackwell!" cried Sophie, her tears forgotten in dismay.

"Yes, he is your choice, isn't he?" said Justin. "I am aware Master Benton didn't approve of him, but quite frankly, I think he was a little prejudiced against the young man." He smiled brightly at Hal, who sat silent. "I know you say his manners need mending, Hal, but intrinsically you think him sound, don't you?"

"I am sure if he suits Mistress Sophie, and time proves his fidelity, we can have no complaints," Hal woodenly agreed.

"No!" said Sophie. "No, no, no! I can't believe you'd say this! You cannot—" she broke off, casting Libby a flustered look. "I will not go against Uncle Edmund's expressed wishes," she said, in a tone to end all argument.

Hal cast down his eyes, hiding a smile, he could see what Justin was at, and was powerless to stop him. Justin had underestimated Sophie if he thought she hadn't understood and taken immediate action to scotch any plot he was hatching to get her married and safely out of the way.

"Oh, I quite thought you liked Adam Blackwell," said Cecily innocently. "He's very handsome—but too tall," she added hastily, as Ned met her eyes, "for my taste, I mean."

"His manners are not those of a gentleman," said Sophie. "And I care nothing for his looks."

"Indeed, according to his stepmother, his manners are already improving daily," said Justin quickly, joining in.

"And once he is happily certain of your affections—" began Ned, aware he'd promised Justin he'd help.

"No," said Sophie bluntly. "No! Not against Uncle Edmund's wishes."

"Well, we shall see," said Justin pacifically. "Let us not get into a disagreement now. Indeed, we must begin to make ourselves ready for the funeral."

⚜

The coffin of Master Benton was borne by his peers, with friends to hold up the pall of black velvet, all wearing black gloves that had been given out by Sophie. Preceded by the Beadle with his long staff, and followed by Sophie, the town council, and all the other mourners carrying sprigs of rosemary, they were met at the doors of the Abbey by two ministers.

The burial service seemed to pass in a nightmare for

Sophie, and all too soon she was following the coffin to a side chapel and seeing it lowered into a vault whilst the mourners filed past to throw in their sprigs of rosemary. She didn't seem able to think properly or clearly anymore. She kept her head lowered and merely curtsied in response to the whispered words of condolence, unable, for the life of her, to get a sound past the huge lump of misery and panic which was rising from her heart to her throat.

"A very good attendance, Sir Henry," remarked Dr Duval, as they paused in the Abbey. "A moving service, too."

"Yes," agreed Hal, who had been wondering during the service where his father and Jacqueline were buried. "Yes, as I understand it, Master Benton's grandfather was one of those who assisted in the purchase of the Abbey from King Henry when all the monks were turned out, and that earned the family the right to be buried here in the Abbey."

"'Tis a beautiful building," agreed the doctor, with a sigh. "It makes me think of my own native Gascony."

"Gascony?" Hal stared in amazement. "You were born in Gascony?"

"Oui," he replied in astonishment. "You are aware, I

think, I am French."

"Well yes," Hal replied. "Although, it is difficult to remember it, you speak English so well."

"I am given to understand you are equally fluent in French," the physician replied with a smile.

So it was, that Ned, approaching in company with Guy some minutes later, was disgusted to hear them deep in conversation in the French tongue. "Hal," he said, eyeing them askance, and waiting for a pause, in what he termed their 'gabbling'. "Hal, will you come and speak to Sophie? She appears almost hysterical, and Libby can do nothing for her."

"Mary thinks you can probably handle her," said Guy, with a grin. "Her faith in you is plainly boundless."

"You are required, mon ami," said the physician with a smile. "We will discuss this further, at a later date."

"Indeed," Hal pressed his hand. "Yes, indeed." He turned, his face alight for the first time in months. "Dr Duval is a native of Gascony," he announced, as he turned back up the central aisle of the abbey. "He knows Auch well."

"Does he?" Ned replied vaguely.

"Auch is the nearest town to where our father died," explained Hal patiently. "Dr Douay, it seems, is in exile, on account of a youthful error. I am—" Hal broke off the sentence as he approached a pillar where Sophie stood, her arms folded on it, weeping copiously, whilst Libby and Mary fluttered about her, and Cecily patted her back ineffectually.

"What, in heaven's name, is going on here?" Hal said sharply. "Libby, Mary, be silent! Pray return at once to the house in company with Guy—you too, Cecily—yes, thank you for your assistance, but Mistress Sophie is going to behave with decorum now! Sophie! Get control of yourself at once, and stop this disgraceful exhibition! This is no conduct befitting a gentlewoman."

"Oh, Hal," she removed her arms, and launched herself into his, as the remainder of his family walked on. "Oh Hal, please don't be cross with me, I am so afraid. Uncle Edmund has looked after me since my own father died when I was a little girl. Who will help me now?"

He held her at arm's length. "I know how lost and alone you must be feeling, Sophie," he said more gently. "Your guardian was more than a father to you. I understand you are afraid of the future, but please do try to stop weeping all the time. Both Justin and I will take care of you. You have no need for concern, you are one of our family now. Did not my wife assure you of it?"

"She doesn't like me Hal," she wept.

"Who can blame her?" he sighed, glancing up over her head as Libby, walking slowly out of the Great Abbey door on Justin's arm, glanced back, her expression one of doubt. He darted her a rueful, comical look, and had the satisfaction of seeing her countenance lift, before he added, in bracing tones: "Come Sophie, please don't embarrass me before the worthy citizens of this town. I am used to the behaviour of well-bred females."

She loosened her frantic hold on his coat and looked up into his face, her own ravaged by grief. "Don't be cold to me, Hal," she implored. "I am not bred like your wife and sisters, to endure all without emotion! I am unhappy and afraid. I don't know what to do for the best!"

"Trust in me," he said firmly, his heart missing a beat as he looked into her lovely, stormy face, and he had to again control his desire to kiss her. "I promise you, you shall not be abandoned. You have my word on it."

"You'll not let them push me into a marriage, to be rid of me, you promise?" she begged, her lovely plump lips trembling.

"My dear, you have no need of my assistance," he replied with a smile. "You check-mated Justin's plan very neatly, I assure you."

"But he frightens me, Hal, he is so ruthless," she whispered, beginning to dry her tears, as she relaxed in his company. "Promise me you'll not allow it. I notice they all obey you."

"I swear to you: I'll not allow you to be coerced into an unsuitable marriage," he replied with a mental sigh, thinking she noticed too much.

"Any marriage," she insisted, anxiety returning to her voice.

"Sophie," he said sadly, shaking his head. "That I cannot do, you must be wed."

"No!" she cried, tears filling her eyes again. "No! Never!"

"Now, don't start to weep again," he said firmly. "Come, we must make haste to join our guests. I'll promise you this: you can have a year free of all plots to marry you, if you so wish, one complete year to grieve, and then we'll discuss the matter anew."

"A year?" she repeated thoughtfully. "A whole year, and you'll tell them it is so? There will be no pushing or plots and plans? A year of peace?"

"Yes," he replied. "If it is your wish." And the thought occurred to him that even Justin couldn't disagree with him in this respect.

"Oh thank you, Hal, thank you," she cried, clasping his arm. "Yes, a year—why, in a year almost anything could happen."

He caught a glimpse of her face as she took the arm he offered, and as they began to walk slowly from the place, a doubt assailed him. A year, he was thinking, would give her time to get over her grief and her infatuation. A year would give them time to find a suitable match for her, and him time to recover.

"Where shall I live?" she asked, as they walked out through the great doors and along the path to the road. They espied Justin and Libby waiting for them at the gate. "I cannot continue to live in Uncle Edmund's house alone."

"No," he agreed. "Not unless we got an older woman to live with you."

"Not Mistress Latham or Mistress Palmer," she said instantly. "I would be driven insane."

"You are very definite in whom won't suit you," he remarked tartly. "Where would you like to live?"

"With you." She replied simply, gazing adoringly at him.

With his wife's eyes on him, he gauged it best to ignore this remark. "Perhaps with my sister Mary at Elmley Park, as you and Cecily are of an age. Then, when she and Ned are wed, you could perhaps accompany them to their home at Rushley Manor," he said mediatively.

"No, I don't think I'd like to live with your sister Mary," she said. "She's kind and lovely, but I want to see you each day."

"We are discussing Sophie's new home," announced Hal, as they joined Justin and Libby. "She doesn't feel she wants to remain here in Chawcester, I am advocating Elmley Park, which is close enough for her to have access to her old friends, and with the added attraction of Cecily being a similar age."

"Would Guy and Mary be willing to take so heavy a charge?" Justin asked, his tones and look indicating his disapproval of Sophie's behaviour. "If she is left to our guardianship, surely she should remain with one of us? Bess and I will be happy for Sophie to make her home with us in Adamsholme."

"No," said Libby simply. "Bess is going to be fully occupied over the next few months, and you have but limited space, Justin. Sophie must come to us at Westwood, where I shall be very glad of her company, especially when Jane marries later in the year. There can be no question but that we have space and enough, and I am sure it is not too far for good friends to make occasional visits."

Justin goggled at his sister, as Sophie exclaimed in delight, and Hal looked dismayed.

"Are you sure, my dear?" he asked, as they all began to walk in the direction of the High Street. "Recollect you have been far from in good health yourself."

"Sophie isn't coming to be a charge upon us, but a dear friend, to live amongst us," said Libby. "She'll enjoy the country, she can learn to ride, and she tells me she loves children. She has to learn how to run a home, too. It will be good for her, and take her mind off her troubles."

"Oh thank you, my lady," cried Sophie, turning back to clasp her hand in passionate gratitude. "You are too good, too kind, you make me feel as if I am not a nuisance to everyone."

Libby patted her hands, a little dismayed at how lovely the girl was. Could she blame Hal for falling for so pretty an animated creature? She seemed artless enough in her emotions, with no hidden shallows, she prayed God Sophie's infatuation was of short duration. "You are not a nuisance at all, child, just a little overwrought —and no wonder with all that's been going on. Now dry your eyes, if you please, and let us hurry to attend to these good people, who have come to help you mourn your Uncle."

Chapter Sixteen

"It shouldn't be much longer now, of course," said Cecily. Under instructions from Justin, she had, with Ned, kept Sophie company all the weary afternoon of the funeral, helping her to give out pairs of gloves and white silk scarves. "Very soon, they'll all be gone, and we'll have the house back to ourselves. Libby was saying you'll be going to Westwood soon, so you'll see Ned often, and us occasionally. Well, next week, I believe, if Hal is back, for we've all been bidden for a feast, to celebrate the anniversary of his and Libby's wedding."

"Yes," said Sophie dully. "He told me he had been married five years nearly." Her head ached with a dull relentless ache. She could see how it was going to be when she got to Westwood. She'd be relegated to the company of Cecily or the children, and never be allowed to spend any time with Hal at all.

"Mistress Cecily, well met!" Giles Durward swept a flourishing bow. "'Tis days since we were last in company! How I have missed your sweet charms! Dear Mistress Sophia!" he turned to her, his eyes glinting. "My poor, dear lady, you have my condolences. I see your heart is heavy indeed, and it can be of little comfort to know we all mourn that good and noble fellow, who was so much more than your guardian. You must feel bereft without his kindly hand to guide you."

"Thank you, sir," she replied, weak tears filling her eyes at his words. "I am indeed heavy of heart, but I try to find consolation in the family of my new guardians."

"New guardians?" he looked aghast. "There is more than one?"

"Indeed," said Ned as she nodded. "My brother, Sir Henry, and my sister's husband Justin Danvers have been named."

"Sir Henry and Mr Danvers! Such new friends to hold so precious a trust," he said. Then, as Ned glared, he added hastily, trying to think desperately: "Good men, indeed. Naturally, one can understand dear Master Benton's reasoning, although, I must confess myself surprised he'd even had time to name new guardians. And it is to these gentlemen, one must apply, one assumes, for the felicity of petitioning for your fair hand, dear, sweet, Mistress Sophia, when you are out of mourning."

"I imagine that is the case," said Sophie. "But I'd not have you put yourself to such trouble, Mr Durward, for my answer will be the same when, or where, you put it."

His smooth smile became set. "Your wishes, dear lady, might not even be consulted," he murmured. "A man doesn't get to be so wealthy as Sir Henry by asking foolish young maids their opinions on marriage."

"Sir Henry has assured me, I need speak to no man of marriage for the next year, Mr Durward," she replied coldly.

"But of course," he agreed. "He'll settle it all himself. I told you, you'll not even be consulted." He laughed at her look of dismayed horror. "Oh don't fret, dear lady, I'll warrant at least one of your suitors will be to your taste."

"If Hal says no marriage will be considered, Sophie, then none will," said Ned soothingly. "Durward is trying to distress you. You'd think, after coming so late to the funeral, he'd be more respectful."

"Late, dear Mr Westwood, not I," Durward replied sharply.

"Yes, you were," said Ned flatly. "I asked Jasper whether you were coming—for you weren't with the Elmley Park people—and he said he'd no idea where you were. Then you slid in the back of the Abbey, and that was after the service had begun."

"I think you'll find you are mistaken, my friend," he said, an edge in his voice. "True, my horse slipped a shoe just short of Chawcester—and I lost time whilst a blacksmith re-nailed it—but I wasn't that late. Now, if you'll excuse me, I do have urgent business with Sir Henry."

"Odious man!" cried Sophie, as he left them rather precipitately.

"Amen to that!" echoed Cecily, as he swiftly quitted the house.

"Oh, I thought you admired some of his qualities," teased Ned. "His ability to recite lines of poetry, his knowledge of herbs and flowers—"

"Even Adam Blackwell picks wild flowers," said Sophie, as Cecily grew red-faced. "If one so very masculine in appearance can do so, I think we can forgive Giles Durward that much?"

"Does Blackwell know his herbs too?" Ned idly asked.

"Well, I don't know," replied Sophie. "I dare say, many are the same, are they not? Like lavender and mallow and rose—" she stopped, as Constable Sambourne pushed through a group of people at the door who were exchanging farewells with Mistress Latham and Mistress Palmer. "What is amiss now?"

"I don't know," Ned turned away, and hastened to join Hal and Guy, as Justin, quickly taking leave of his cousins, came up.

"You are sure, man?" Hal was saying, his voice echoing his disbelief.

"The Bailiff sent me to fetch you, sir," he replied. "He said, sorry as to disturb the wake, like, but he'd appreciate your opinion on the matter."

"And he'd been hit on the head, too?" said Hal.

"Aye, and pushed through his own loft with his barrels. Mind, that's what has Mr Keeble worried. I mean, he's been bobbing about in the Avon all afternoon, along with them there barrels. No wonder he's battered and bruised."

"Who is it?" asked Justin. Then, as Hal glanced coldly to him, he said: "Oh dear God, not Will Greenway?"

"Yes," hissed Hal. "Will Greenway. Yet another dead because of your insistence on getting to the truth! I told you, there comes a time to let sleeping dogs lie! But no, you must know best! How many more must die before you are satisfied? All those on your lists? Is that the way to find the murderer? He's the only one left alive?"

❧

Chapter Seventeen

Sophie glanced over her shoulder as she softly pulled the door closed behind her. Hal and Justin had departed, very tight-lipped, for the Bailiff's house. Mary and Guy had left for home with both Durwards. Libby had retired to her chamber to rest, and Ned and Cecily were in the garden, squabbling over the names of flowers in the soft twilight.

They expected her to join them there and help in their wooing, but the prospect filled her with misery. Not for her, the happy role of a betrothed bride, dallying in a pleasant bower with her lover, no, her story was quite different. She knew she'd never coax Hal into a shady garden to exchange caresses. If they embraced at all, it was because he was driven to it, and the hasty, explosive nature of his kisses were the only memory she would ever have of him. She knew she deserved no better, she was wicked in desiring another woman's husband. She should not, therefore, expect any happiness in her sin, yet, try as she did, she could not turn away from him. And if she couldn't be with him, she'd sooner be alone. She slipped down the High Street, hugging the shadows, glad of the cooler air as she turned to the river.

She'd walk on the Common, she decided, gather a few more of the sweet primroses which grew there, and take them to the Abbey to lay on Uncle Edmund's grave. She was surprised at how much she already missed him, missed his step on the stair, his deep cheery voice, the splendid calmness which always enveloped her when he was near.

Now there was only Hal, and he didn't make her feel calm. The sight of him made her tingle, the sound of his voice made her heart leap, and the thought of his touch made all her senses come alive. If only she could be in his arms, know she was safe from all harm, this anxiety might go. But she knew it was useless, they were going to keep her from him, she could tell. He was constantly surrounded by one or another of his family, and she feared she'd never be alone with him again.

She crossed the river by the mill and walked onto the Common amongst the grazing beasts. Adam had told her the flowers grew on the far side, away from the sheep where the trees formed a belt at King Henry's hill. Humming a dismal tune to herself, she made her way across the open land, occasionally picking a piece of wool from the hedgerow and pulling it asunder. These were her sheep, she knew that from their markings. She was, she supposed, a wealthy young woman, but what wouldn't she give to be but a poor shepherdess, going home to her true love.

She forced herself to think again about Adam and his devotion, and grew to wondering, in a morass of self-pity, if in a year's time, she'd be too old and ugly for him to even consider. A whole year seemed forever to Sophie. A few hours seemed an eternity without Hal. She'd collect her flowers, put them on Uncle Edmund's grave, and then call at the Bailiff's house. Like as not, Hal would be returning home, and she could walk in his company. True, Justin would be there, but she had a premonition Justin would always be there, deliberately setting them apart.

Then, as if the wish were father to the thought, she beheld Adam standing before her. "Oh, Adam, what a shock you gave me!" she cried.

"Sorry Sophie," he said quickly. "I didn't mean to

for at least a year," she said with a sigh, a little tempted by this avowal of his love.

"A year!" he cried indignantly.

"Yes," she said, glancing to him. "I said I was so confused and unhappy, so Sir Henry said I need not even consider the question of marriage until I am out of mourning. He said a genuine suitor would be content to wait."

"Not content," said Adam, smiling a little. "Agreeable—if that's what you truly wanted—but never content."

"Now I am not sure," she sighed. "Yesterday—earlier, even—I wanted to think of nothing. But now, my life seems so empty, so devoid of all purpose. It is as if I am condemned to limbo for a year, I don't know what to think."

"I think you are probably too tired and overwrought to think any more about it at present," Adam said kindly. "Tomorrow, after you've slept, you'll feel differently, and by this time next week, perhaps different again. Don't make too hasty a decision."

"Dear Adam," she smiled vaguely at him, and clasped his arm absently. "You are so good to me. I wish—oh I wish, I could lay my troubles on your shoulders and be free of them."

"They are broad enough, and willing," he said stoutly, for in truth, she was more inclined to his suit this evening, than at any time since the spring. "Oh Sophie, do say yes, I'll wait if you want, but I'll wait happier, if only you'd say yes now!"

"I can't, Adam," she replied, true regret in her voice. "I'd like to be able to say yes. To cast everything to the four winds, and throw in my lot with yours. But I can't. It wouldn't be fair to me, and it wouldn't be fair to you. Sir Henry is right, I need time to think, to settle matters in my own mind."

"I don't care about being fair to me—" he began, but she interrupted him quickly.

"Oh, do be a dear, Adam, and don't dispute with me," she begged. "I am so weary and sick at heart, I just want to be alone!"

He saw the sense of this, and his conscience twinged. "I beg pardon, my dear," he said gently. "You're right, I shouldn't tease you when you're so sad, but I can't leave you like this. Come, allow me to escort you home."

"No, for I have gathered these for Uncle Edmund's grave, and I hear the Abbey clock strike the hour. You have your tasks. I'll just walk across to the Abbey and lay these on his grave, and then I'll go home."

"You shouldn't be out like this unescorted," he said. "I'm surprised Sir Henry allows it."

"He doesn't," she sighed, "but I felt the need to be alone. You must go, Adam. Mistress Blackwell will be waiting."

"Mind you go straight home," he said frowning, as he clasped her hand in farewell. "Don't linger, now."

"I won't," she replied, but for all that, she picked a dozen more of the fragile blooms whose colour so aptly mirrored her hair, and had turned back to look at the Abbey, surprised at how quickly the light was fading, when the rider came into view.

At first, she thought, as he made straight for her, it was Hal, and her heart leapt at the idea of him sweeping her up into his arms and riding off into the night with her. But then, she realised he was heavier than Hal, and in that second, she recognised Giles Durward. She stood, shielding her eyes against the setting sun as she cried: "Is ought amiss, Mr Durward? Is somebody else killed?" she cried, her anxiety surfacing.

"You must come at once!" he cried, his horse slithering to a halt beside her, as he extended an imperious hand.

"What is wrong?" she cried in dismay, placing her tiny foot on his spurred boot and being hoisted into the saddle before him. "Is it Mistress Armstrong? Not Lady Westwood! Oh pray God, not Hal himself!"

"Be still," he said roughly. "And let us quickly get there." He spun his horse about and set its head in the direction of Chipping Barbury.

"Where are we going?" she cried, as his arms clamped her to him, and the horse took off as if it had wings.

"Lamton," he replied, the wind taking his voice. "I've a farm there."

"Lamton!" she cried. "Why? What? Please, Mr Durward! Giles! What—"

"Be silent!" he snarled, as her voice rose in panic. He reined in a little as the riverbank came in sight and allowed the horse to pick its way down the bank more temperately.

"But why? Giles, let me go! This cannot—you can't mean to—ahh!" This last exclamation came as he guided the horse into the river and the water rose to their thighs.

"Are you mad?" she shrieked. "Let me go at once! Ahh!" She gave a shriek of pain as he hit her with the back of his hand, making her reel in the saddle.

"Now be silent!" he snarled, his voice a warning growl. "Not another sound, or I'll take steps to stop your mouth!"

She whimpered in fear as the blood from her nose splashed onto her gown, and she tasted the salt in her mouth. "Where are we going?" she whispered, as the horse clambered up the far bank.

"I've told you, to my house near Lamton. I've a farm just over the border."

"Why?" she cried, although she already knew the answer.

"To spend some time in each other's company," he replied grinning with malice. "That's right, my dear, by the time I've finished with you, you'll be begging me to marry you!"

He laughed as she gave a moan of terror, and kicking his horse, setting off across country again.

❧

Chapter Eighteen

"I tell you this," said Hal, as he and Justin entered the house again. "If that's what passes as investigating the matter, I'm surprised anyone is ever brought to justice in this town."

"I think some of your ideas were rather new to both the Bailiff and the constable," remarked Justin, unable to repress a grin.

"You mean, like checking the testimony of the witnesses?" Hal raised his eyes to heaven.

"I don't think it had ever occurred to either of them before, though," chuckled Justin. "Oh, I know I shouldn't laugh. It's a serious matter, but Sambourne could indeed be a model for Dogberry."

Hal stared at him for a moment, his irritation fading. "You're right, he is the man himself!" he cried, laughter bubbling up inside him. "One can almost hear the words on his lips!"

Justin laughed heartily with him, and then glanced up, as Ned came quickly down the stairs. "Is she with you?" he asked, his young face filled with anxiety. "We've only just missed her. We've searched the house, but she's nowhere to be found. Is she not with you? Cecily was sure she'd have come to meet you!"

"Who? Sophie?" Justin cried frowning.

"Sophie?" Hal asked sharply. "Do you say she is missing?"

"Yes. Cecily and I were in the garden, we—we didn't notice the passing of time until dusk. We thought she'd join us there, you see. But as the moon was rising, we realised she hadn't. And, we came to—well, look for her."

"How long has she been gone?" Hal cried quickly.

"Not long," said Cecily, her face white, as she followed Ned down the stairs. "Not much more than an hour."

"You are certain she is not in the house?" Justin asked sharply.

"No, definitely not. We've searched from attics to cellars," said Ned. "She hasn't taken her horse, as she's not allowed to ride without a groom. We thought perhaps she came to meet you and Justin."

"Ned, go into the kitchen, see if any saw her go," said Hal. "She may indeed have slipped out for a breath of air. But where would she go?"

"She has no companions of her own age, not now the Mayor's daughter is wed. She told me so," said Justin. "To see my cousin Eunice, or Mistress Latham?"

"It's not likely, although possible, I suppose," said Hal doubtfully, "if she wanted to talk to an older woman."

"She may have followed Mary and Guy to Elmley Park?" suggested Cecily, following his train of thought.

"Why for?" asked Justin blankly. "She has taken no horse, and it is getting dark."

"Well, to, see Giles Durward?" she suggested tentatively. "He—he has been speaking of marriage again."

"She can't abide the fellow," said Justin dismissively.

Ned came running back from the kitchen. "None saw her go, but Cook said she used sometimes to walk on the Common, to meet Adam Blackwell at twilight."

"I'll go and see," said Hal, his hand on the door.

"Wait!" Justin said. "I'll go with you to my cousin's house, just in case. Ned, take a horse and ride out towards Elmley, just in case she did anything so foolish as to set off on foot at this time of night."

"She may have done," he agreed. "She was in very low spirits this afternoon. I'll get my horse."

"Cecily, you stay here in case she returns or Libby wakes up," continued Justin. "Right then, we'll each go our separate ways. It will be quicker!"

He followed Hal, who was halfway down the street, calling: "I'll join you on the Common, once I've spoken to Eunice."

Hal raised his hand in acknowledgement, and plunged down the alley he'd used before leading to the river. He quickly found the boatman he'd met previously just putting his boat away, and hailed him.

"Mistress Sophia Redcroft," the boatman replied. "Aye, I saw her earlier, walking way over the other side of the wood."

"She didn't come back by boat?" Hal asked, looking concerned.

"No, now you mention it, she didn't," he said. "Unless she crossed by the mill—but no, the water's higher now, she couldn't have done." He frowned. "I seem to remember a horseman, too," he said. "Over in that direction."

"Adam Blackwell?" demanded Hal sharply. He was rather amazed at the sudden murderous surge of jealously which had filled his breast on the mention of Adam's name.

"No, he'll be serving ale at this time of night," the boatman returned. "No, another fellow, I've seen him hereabouts. He's one of the new folk at Elmley Park. The one that dresses like a fool!"

"Giles Durward!" Hal snarled through clenched teeth. Then, recollecting the earlier words of Guy, he demanded: "Tell me, what is in that direction?"

"Over the other side of the Severn?" the boatman asked, surprised. "Well, Herefordshire and the borders, isn't it?"

"Lamton?" Hal cried in dismay, his worst fears confirmed.

"Yes," replied the man. "Lamton is in that general direction."

"Quick, man, where can I get a horse?" Hal demanded. "It is imperative I have a horse at once."

"Well, my neighbour grazes his young cob on the Common," said the man. "But he's only half broken, and there's no saddle—"

"That will do. Time is of the essence," Hal produced a handful of coins, which he dropped into the amazed boatman's cap. "Row me across, I beg, and then go tell your neighbour I've hired his horse." The boatman goggled, but pushed the boat back into the water obligingly. Hal leapt aboard and vaulted onto the far bank, before the boatman had time to tie up. "If my brother comes looking for me, tell him I am gone to Lamton," he shouted over his shoulder.

"Do you want help with the cob?" called the man. "It's that one, tethered there."

"I'll manage, thank you," Hal called back.

"Have a care, he'll be frisky, he's not been ridden in three days," returned the boatman with a shrug.

The cob, who was eyeing Hal with suspicion, came surprisingly easily to hand in hope of oats, and even disappointed, allowed him to mount, only shying slightly. Hal doubled the rope over, to form makeshift reins, and gave him a gentle kick. The horse responded by taking a few uncertain steps. Hal kicked harder and he broke into a half-hearted trot. Using the rope, he slapped at the horse's rump and finally got a response. The cob cantered easily across the hummocky grass, his ears on the prick, ready for an adventure.

⚜

Chapter Nineteen

Sophie tried desperately to stop the shuddering of her body. She didn't want him to know how afraid she was. She kept trying to think of a plan of what to do, of how to outwit this awful man, but her brain wouldn't cooperate. Over and over in her mind, she was crying out for Hal to come. Hal to help her. Hal to rescue her from the consequences of her own folly.

She closed her eyes, as the horse stumbled again, it was growing weary, she could tell. He was carrying the double weight and worst still, the moonlight which had been so helpful at first, was now becoming dim, as a mist began to rise in the fields.

Giles pulled the horse to a halt, scowling ahead in the dimness, and once again Sophie shut her eyes, rather than see his dark saturnine face so close to hers. Then, as he grunted in satisfaction, she saw a light flickering and a huddle of buildings. She held herself ready, determined if it was a village or even only a hamlet, to cry out, so that someone might know her plight, and possibly come to her aid. But to her despair, as they drew closer, she could see it was but a farm and outbuildings.

Durward unhitched the gate and rode into the yard, shouting for his servant. He slid from the saddle, dragging Sophie with him.

"Denton!" he bellowed. "Get out here, and take this horse."

The man Sophie had seen at Elmley Park slipped from a barn and came to take the bridle, casting Sophie a curious look, as he led the exhausted beast away.

"Did you do as I bid you?" Giles demanded.

"Aye, sir, I did," the servant agreed and made haste to be gone.

"Come then, my lovely," Giles continued, dragging her forward. "Your bower awaits you."

"Giles," she panted, resisting him with all her strength. "Giles, if you want my money, you can have it, I care nothing for it, I'll give all my money to you! I'll sign anything, I swear! Just let me go!"

He laughed at this. "You sweet innocent, I'll have all your money anyway—and you." His laughter increased at her groan of horror. "And do you know, I'll enjoy that the most!"

"Very well!" As he pushed her over the threshold, Sophie caught at the doorpost. "Very well, Giles I'll agree to marry you, I give my word, I'll marry you as soon as I am able, but for pity's sake, have mercy! I only buried my Uncle this afternoon!"

He forced her hands from the doorway, ripping her fingernails, and clasped her upper arms in a vicious grip. "You sing a different tune now, Sophie, I see," he hissed, his face very close to hers, so that she could smell his sour breath. "I'll have you here and now, and then we'll be married when I choose."

She shut her eyes to blot out his flushed, lecherous features, her head swimming with fear, and almost dropped where she stood as he released her to bolt the door.

"Yes! Denton hasn't done too badly," Giles remarked, stripping off his hat and gloves and throwing them to the table, as he glanced about the candlelit room. Sophie staggered to a wooden bench and sat down, her legs no longer able to hold her.

"Oh no, my dear, draw near the fire, dry your feet and legs. We don't want you catching a chill, do we?" he said, forcing her to a settle drawn close to a small fire. He knelt at her feet, removing her sodden shoes and lifting her wet skirts to loosen her garters.

She gave a cry of fear and horror, which only made him laugh, and catch the hand which went to prevent him, bending back her fingers in so painful a manner that she shrieked again, tears filling her eyes. "I told you Sophie, I will have you," he said, with deliberate menace in his voice. "I can do this my way, and you'll not get hurt, or you can try to stop me, and I'll hurt you more than you can imagine."

She swallowed, tears beginning to trickle down her cheeks, her heart pounding. She felt sick with the horror of him. Desperately, as he released her garter and stroked her thigh before rolling down her stocking, she looked about her, and espying a jug of wine and two mugs on the table, whispered: "A drink, I need a drink. I am cold, and my throat is dry."

"Seeking Dutch courage?" he sneered, kissing her knee as he removed her other stocking. "Very well, I'll get you some wine. You get your gown off."

"My gown?" she cried, folding her arms across her chest.

"Why do you think I've brought you here to this isolated spot?" he asked, going over to the table to pour two cups of wine. Then, as she didn't answer, but only stared at him in mute terror, he laughed again. "That's right, so I can enjoy you! Here, drink this down, and don't look so tragic. You never know, you might like it!"

She sipped the wine as he sat down to pull off his own wet boots. His stockings, coat and waistcoat followed. Then, as he picked up his cup of wine, he said sharply: "I told you to take you clothes off! Now!"

She jumped and spilt a little of the wine, choking on it, too, but as he moved to hit her, she hastened to her feet, quickly unlacing her bodice.

He sprawled back in the chair, his eyes never leaving her face. "Continue!" he commanded, as she slid out of her wet clinging skirts, and stood in her petticoats. The bodice followed and the petticoat, so that she was revealed in a fine linen shift.

"That too, I'll have you naked," he said, his words slurred with mingled drink and desire.

She bent to lift the hem, despair in her heart, when the sound of a horse came to their ears.

"You there!" Hal's voice came like the answer to a prayer. "Where the devil am I? Is it far to Lamton?"

"Hal!" Sophie screamed at the top of her voice. "Hal, help me!"

"Be silent!" Durward shouted, and flew at her, hitting her with his upraised fist.

She fell to the floor dazed, as a thundering came upon the door. "Sophie!" shouted Hal. "Sophie are you there?"

"Go away Westwood!" cried Durward, snatching up his sword. "You are spoiling my enjoyment of your ward!"

Furious oaths came in reply to this taunt, as the door rocked under Hal's assault. Sophie, regaining some of her senses, saw Giles advancing on the door, his sword held ready as he unbolted it.

"Hal, have a care, he is—" she screamed, as Hal, distaining the door, threw himself through the casement of the window, scattering wood and glass all over the floor. Hal staggered to his feet, his cheek and neck bleeding.

His initial shock at Hal's entry over, Durward advanced on him, his sword glinting evilly. "Oh, splendid! Now I get the chance to kill you too, Westwood," Giles cried, his eyes flashing with murderous light. "No, in fact, I'll not kill you right off, I'll let you bleed to death, like I did that prattling preacher, and you can watch as

I have your precious ward. Die watching it!"

Giles laughed in manner to suggest he'd lost all sense and circled on Hal, who was holding his hand to the cut on his cheek which bled freely and eyeing his opponent doubtfully.

Hal knew he was in a desperate situation. He dodged the first lunge, spinning about on the balls of his feet, his eyes going to Sophie, taking in her bleeding and bruised face. Fury rose in him that this man could so hurt her, and in that moment, he knew he'd kill him with his bare hands if need be. "Come on, Durward," his fury making his voice shake. "Come on, try fighting a man, rather than a defenceless girl!"

Durward gave a roar of anger, and leapt for him as Sophie got to her feet. Her head was still reeling, but she could see Hal was unarmed. She darted a frantic look about her for a weapon to throw him, and saw only the log basket. As Durward ripped the sleeve of Hal's coat in a feint and drew blood, she panicked, snatched up a heavy log, and not giving herself time to think, launched herself across the room, swinging it to crash down on Giles Durward's head with a sickening thud.

❧

Chapter Twenty

Giles Durward gave an odd grunt, his knees buckled, and his sword clattered on the flagstones as he crumpled on a heap.

"Sweet Jesus! Have I killed him?" Sophie whispered the words in horror.

"I hope not, for I fully intend to!" Hal cried, still filled with wrath as he dropped to his knees beside the still figure, mechanically catching up the sword. Gingerly, he turned the body over, noting with a feeling of fleeting dismay how the head flopped back in a telltale manner. His fingers sought the pulse at Giles's neck, as he doubtfully noted how blood oozed from the shattered skull, soaking into his hair. For just a second, something fluttered under the pressure of Hal's fingers, and then was gone.

Hal looked up into her whitened face. "He's dead,"

he said, his hand going to wipe away the blood on his cheek.

She dropped the log, swaying uncertainly, so that he was forced to leap to his feet to catch her into his arms.

"Sophie! Sophie?" he cried. "Oh, you poor child, are you hurt? Did he harm you?" Over the top of her tangled hair, his eyes took in the various items of her clothing and feared the worst.

She shuddered convulsively, and then screamed as the servant appeared at the ruin of the window, his face pale and full of fear.

"Halt, you!" Hal cried, advancing on him with his sword at the ready. The man took one look at his master dead and ran.

"Sit down a moment, my sweet," soothed Hal, half-carrying her to the settle. "I'll just check there are no more of them."

"No, Hal," she moaned. "Don't leave me, I beg you, don't leave me. There was only Giles and his man!"

The clatter of hooves on the cobbles told them the servant was making good his escape. Hal darted to the door, opening it. "Damn him, has he taken the horses?" he cried.

"Hal, I beg you, don't leave me with that thing," she wailed, pointing to the body.

"He can do you no more harm," he replied. "Look, I should stable my horse, it seems that fellow has only taken his own, and Durward's."

"Hal, please!" she wept, her voice breaking.

"Oh well, he's lame anyway, he probably won't go far," said Hal, seeing how overwrought she was. A feeling of lassitude was creeping over him, he shook his head to clear it, and added: "But I think we'll get rid of this first."

He crossed to grab Durward's body by the heels and pulled it across the flagstones, suppressing a groan at the pain this caused his wounded arm. In desperation, he yanked the body out the door and left it in the yard.

He returned, shutting the door and throwing the bolt across. His steps swayed a little as he suddenly felt faint. He crossed to the shattered window and, using his good arm, swept aside the glass before releasing the shutters and bolting them in place.

"There now," he stumbled to the bench, his legs shaky. "At least we are safe, even if he should go for help." He swallowed and shut his eyes against a momentary dizziness. "Sophie," he said faintly. "Do you feel up to pouring me a drink, and then perhaps binding up this arm for me? It's bleeding steadily and making me feel faint."

She gave a cry of horror and flew to his side. "Hal, I had forgotten you were wounded!" she cried out in dismay, as she noticed the blood. "Let me look—oh sweet Jesus! He has nearly lain your arm open to the bone."

"Hardly," he weakly chuckled. "'Tis a mere scratch, but a damned painful one." He struggled out of his coat. "Rip my shirtsleeve out if you can, and we'll try to bind the wound with it."

"No, indeed," she cried. "It is soaked in blood already. I'll use my petticoat, it's only slightly damp now."

He watched as she took up Durward's sword and used it to make a cut in her petticoat, ripping it further between her teeth into a long strip, and rolling it to form a bandage.

"Hold the edges of the flesh together, Hal," she commanded, as the blood welled again after she'd wiped it away with his dampened handkerchief. "I'll bind it tightly."

"Not too tightly," he warned. "Otherwise it'll throb. Yes, that's about right."

"What about your cheek? That is a flesh wound,"

she said looking at it. "It has almost stopped bleeding now."

"That's probably because I've not got a lot of blood left!" he said with a shaky laugh. Then, as she laughed too, and looked into his eyes, he sobered saying quietly: "Did he harm you?"

"Yes, but not in the way you mean," she said, her voice trembling. "He hit me, and made my nose bleed, and frightened me. But he didn't take me. He was too intent in humiliating me by making me strip naked to get that far. But if you hadn't come when you did…" she stopped as tears welled over again, and slid willy-nilly down her cheeks and nose.

"Don't weep, 'tis over now. He'll never frighten you again," he soothed. "Come, sit with me by the fire. Throw that log on. I am cold."

She did as he bid, first fetching him a cup of wine, which they shared. Then, he pulled her close to his side, slipping his arm about her and hugging her.

"Can you bear to tell me what happened?" he asked gently.

"When you and Justin left, I felt so suddenly alone," she said, leaning her head against his shoulder, and letting go a long shuddering sigh. "I had a vision of my life stretching out before me, never being allowed to be with you. Seeing you only in the company of others, and I have never felt so alone and miserable. So, I thought I'd walk to the Common to pick some wild flowers—"

"And to meet Adam Blackwell?" he suggested sharply.

"No," she replied quickly. "That is, yes, I did meet him, but not by appointment as I used to do. I haven't done so in days. I went to pick flowers for Uncle Edmund to put on his grave, and indeed was picking then still, Adam having left, when Giles Durward came riding across the Common. I don't know why, but I immediately assumed something was wrong."

"Well, there have been four murders in as many days," he remarked. "It seemed to me as soon as we paused for breath, someone rushes in and announces another body!"

She gave a shaky laugh, relieved that he hadn't thought her foolish. "I remember wondering who was taken ill, —or worse—but he—he just put down his hand to me, and commanded me to go, and like an fool, I did."

"Sophie, Sophie!" he cried in dismay. "Did not Justin warn you have a care of him?"

"Yes, and had he been smiling and full of fat compliments, I wouldn't have trusted him an inch," she agreed. "But he seemed so grim and anxious, that I was certain something dreadful had happened."

"Which it had, as soon as he had you on that horse," said Hal.

"Yes," she sighed. "It wasn't until he rode the horse at the Severn, that I realised something was amiss. I cried out for him to let me go, but we plunged into the river and that took my breath away and made me scream. It was then that he first hit me."

She was silent for a few moments, and he hugged her tightly. "None had ever hurt me before," she whispered. "It was a shock and it frightened me—truly frightened me. It froze me, both bodily and my thoughts. I knew I should do something to help myself. That I should think of a clever plan to get free of him, but all my silly head would say, over and over again, was: Hal, help me! And you did."

"Only by pure chance," he said, resting his head on top of her curls as he hugged her again. "I went looking for you on the Common, and met up with Owen the boatman. He said he'd seen you, and then remembered Giles. I immediately feared the worst. I took a half-tamed horse, which was useful in a way, for he knew no fear, and went like the wind. But I became hopelessly lost. I only knew the general direction Durward had taken, and that he'd recently evicted some tenants near Lamton. I just rode on, hoping to find the village and ask directions. Then, the mist came down, and I thought I was finished, until I saw the light of the farm. I had no idea. I rode into the yard with my poor horse suddenly going lame. I was hoping to borrow another, and get some directions. If that man of Giles Durward had had his wits about him, I'd have never even heard your voice."

"I was never more thankful than to hear yours," she said, holding him close. "I thought I was finished, and then, when I was calling to you with all my thought, I heard you call out in reply."

"I couldn't believe it. Then, when Durward replied, I was filled with fury. I never liked the fellow, and I wanted to kill him. Do you know, I don't even remember getting through the window, just the pain as I cut my cheek and hit the floor."

"I felt certain he'd kill you," she whispered, the terror in her voice again. "I didn't think. I just knew you needed a sword, and there wasn't one! So, I picked up the log and hit him with it. It was horrid when he went down like that!"

"But something of a relief. I'd no sword and he'd already cut my arm open," Hal remarked.

"What shall we do?" she asked, hiding her face in his waistcoat. "Shall I have to stand trial for murder?"

"No," he replied. "In fact, as you'd not even like having to talk of it publicly, we'll say I did it. We were both in danger, he was clearly mad, so I defended us as best I could."

"He was mad wasn't he, Hal?" she asked after a few moments. "He killed that poor preacher Sam Hedges, didn't he?"

"Not only him, but all of them, Sophie," he replied. "Justin said he knew it was him, but hadn't enough proof."

"Uncle Edmund, too?" she asked in horror.

"Yes, he poisoned him with the hemlock he picked when out walking with Cecily. Don't you recall her saying he knew all the herbs, and that they'd walked by the river?"

She nodded, and then asked miserably: "All those deaths, just to get my money?"

Once again, her held her close, recognising the horror in her voice. "He was mad," he repeated, "remember that. He'd become insane in his desire to marry you and take possession of your money. You are in no way to blame."

"Justin will think I am," she whispered. "It was to stop Giles, that he wanted me to become betrothed to Adam."

"Not completely," he replied. "Justin is a good man, but he has family feeling like us all. His intention is to protect his sister. And I think, personally, Durward was too far gone. I think an announcement of your betrothal to Adam Blackwell would have had the same result, he'd have tried to kidnap you all the same. Only that Adam might have found himself on trial for murder, for Adam most surely would have killed Durward."

She gave an unsteady chuckle, and then began to weep quietly and hopelessly into his waistcoat. He let her sob out all her despair and terror for some while, as he sat stroking her golden curls, then as she showed signs of recovery, he gave her the remains of the cup of wine.

"I'm sorry, I don't appear to have a clean handkerchief about me today," he said, with a grimace of a smile.

"No, I used it to bathe your wound," she said, wiping her face with her hands, and taking the wine. She sipped it distastefully. "Anyway, I'm glad," she added. "I'd sooner not be patronised by you in a superior mood."

He smiled at the flash of her old spirit, but his brow creased as she fell to weeping again.

"Oh Hal, Hal, what shall we do?" she wept. "What is to become of me?"

"I've told you, we'll stay here tonight," he replied wearily. "In a moment, you might look at that bed by the chimney and see if you can't snatch a few hour's sleep. Then, once this mist lifts at dawn, we'll set out on our way back to Chawcester."

"On a lame horse, with you injured?" she replied, sniffing.

"Well, I think he only sprained something, he might be recovered enough by the morning to take your weight," he said reasonably. "I can walk. 'Tis no more than what—eight, ten miles?"

"Nearer twelve," she said. "And I'll not ride an injured beast. I can walk and lead him, poor fellow, but what of you?"

"This is the merest scratch," he replied valiantly. "I shall do well enough."

She glanced to him, doubt in her eyes. "Shall you?" she asked, then as he smiled his glinting smile nodding, her despair washed over her again and she wept anew. "Besides, Hal, you knew that's not what I meant," she said. "I meant, what will become of me?"

He stroked her hair from her face tenderly. "I do not know," he replied softly. "I have given you my word you shall have a year of mourning, and my wife has said you shall live with us at Westwood. Further than that, I cannot see. Time is a great healer, Sophie. I know, you've heard that from every adult since you could first comprehend, but it is one of life's great truisms. The facts are, that things which are barely tolerable today, six months hence, are often healed over."

"If you mean that I shan't love you in six months, Hal, you are wrong!" she cried passionately, through her tears.

"No, I don't mean that," he said in soothing tones. He was well aware that to suggest to someone in the sharp pangs of their first love affair that the passion might dim was tactless. "I mean that you've had to endure many shocks and grief this past few months, and that a period of quiet reflection may well assist you in bringing everything into better perspective."

"Now you begin to sound like Justin again," she cried pouting. "Don't you understand that nothing, nothing, will ever change how I love you!"

His arms tightened about her and he kissed the top of her tousled head. "Yes, I understand that very well," he said softly. "But you must understand also, that I cannot love you. I am a married man, I have a duty to my wife and family."

"And no room in your heart for me?" she asked piteously.

"My dear, my darling," he murmured. "At present, my heart is full of you, but," he added quickly, as hope filled her eyes, "you are an intelligent woman, you cannot want me to disgrace myself before my friends and family. I cannot love you in the way you want. I'll love you as a sister with all my heart. I'll take care of you and see you want for nothing. But I cannot love you as a lover."

"Oh Hal!" she cried, hiding her face in his waistcoat again. "Must you be so noble?"

"Yes, I'm afraid I must!" he sighed. "But come, enough of these tears now, I think you should try to get some sleep. See if that bed is acceptable."

She glanced at it and shuddered. "I'd sooner stay here

with you. It looks alive to me."

"Yes," he agreed with a sigh. "You are probably right. However, I think if you are to remain here with me, you'd better put on some of your clothes that aren't torn to strips to make bandages or still damp from the river. Bustle about, do, and set up my coat to dry, if you will."

"What shall I do with Giles's clothes?" she asked, as she put more logs on the fire, and then put a stool in front of it to take his coat, and her damp stockings.

"Throw them in a heap somewhere," he replied. He eased himself into a more comfortable position, and wondered if it was the wine that Giles had supplied that was so strong, or if he was light-headed with loss of blood.

Quickly, she scrambled into her shortened petticoats and her bodice, taking her gown to finish drying alongside his coat. "Your boots are still wet, Hal, and your stockings," she said. "You'll take a chill if you sleep the night in them. Let me take them off for you."

"Can you manage?" he asked, as she bent at his feet to do so. "I'm sorry, I feel so cursed weak. It must be all the blood I lost. Is there another cup of wine?"

She hurried to fetch it for him, having put his boots

and stockings to steam gently on the hearth. "I don't think my boots will ever be the same again," he remarked with a dispassionate air, as she dried his feet on Giles's elegant velvet waistcoat.

"Do you think anything will?" she asked in reply.

"Yes, oh yes," he said in soothing tones. "Yes, you'd be surprised how soon this will all fade away. Come, that will do now, settle down here and try to get some sleep, I have a feeling tomorrow will be a very long day."

Chapter Twenty-One

In spite of Hal's conviction that he'd never close his eyes all night in his uncomfortable position on the hard settle, it was the sound of voices in the yard which roused him shortly after dawn the next morning.

In a moment, he was on his feet, pushing the sleeping Sophie from his arms, swaying with weakness as he snatched up Giles Durward's fallen sword. He stood listening intently, fearing it was Denton returned, and then relaxed as he caught the grave tones of Justin's voice.

"Don't be afraid," he said, as Sophie stared at him in dismay. "It's Justin. And it sounds as if our friends have arrived. I'll go out to meet them whilst you make yourself tidy."

He stumbled forward, rather surprised at how unsteady his legs felt and unbolted the door, opening it upon Justin, bent over Durward's damp body, with Sambourne the constable and Ned behind him.

"Hal, thank God," Ned said. Then, his eyes took in Hal's blood-stained sleeve. "Are you hurt?"

"A scratch from our friend, but it bled a lot," Hal replied, stepping over the body, and closing the door on Sophie. He was glad to feel the cool morning air on his face.

"He's dead, Hal," said Justin, who'd moved away and now stood next to Ned, surveying him doubtfully.

"Yes, I know, I put him there," replied Hal, staggering a little, as the fresh air hit him. "I'm sorry, but I didn't care to spend the night with a corpse."

"Who killed him?" asked Justin, as Ned caught Hal's sound arm, steadying him. "Are you ill, Hal?"

"Devil a bit," he replied, with a sharp laugh. "I don't know, but my legs feel like jelly." He leaned heavily on Ned's shoulder, and met Justin's eyes. "I killed him, before he killed me and ravished Sophie."

"Sophie, is she harmed?" asked Justin, glancing to the shut farmhouse door.

"She's battered and bruised, and has probably taken a chill from being half-drowned in the river, but apart from being near hysterical from terror, she appears to have taken no lasting harm from Durward," he replied, shuddering as sweat began to pour down his face.

"Thank God for that," said Justin. "I feared the worst when we couldn't find her. How came you to find her? And why didn't you return home? You must have guessed we'd be mad with worry."

"The mist came down as I got here. Finding this place was the merest chance. I was looking for information, and possibly a horse, as mine had gone lame galloping over rough terrain. Is he about, do you know?" Hal looked round the yard vaguely, feeling strangely dislocated from the scene, as if he were taking part in a play and couldn't quite recollect the words.

"I'll go and look for him," said Ned. "He can't have gone far. But surely you should go back inside, Hal, you've a fever, you can barely stand."

"I'll do well enough, help me to the mounting block, there's a good fellow. Sophie's making herself ready," he replied, anxious they should not burst in on her until she should be ready to face them.

"I'll go and help the young master," said the constable, eyeing Hal oddly. "We'll need another mount to carry back the corpse."

"How comes it that Durward is dead, Hal?" Justin

asked sharply, as Ned and the constable walked off towards the barn.

"I got here to find Durward and Sophie. He'd abducted her, as you thought he might, and brought her
here, to force her to consent to marriage with him," Hal
leaned his head back against the stone of the wall to
keep it from spinning. "I arrived in time to prevent his
intention, but he took issue with my interference and
tried to kill me. I was a little stunned by my entrance —
I went through that window in fine style—and before I
knew it, the fellow had gone for my sword arm and laid
it open. A fine rescuer, to be incapacitated so easily! Unfortunately, I was bleeding steadily and Durward was in
no mood for discussion, so I dispensed with finesse. I
snatched up a log from the hearth, and hit him over the
head with it."

"You hit an armed man over the head?" said Justin
frowning, and as ever, seizing upon the one fact which
was out of place.

"Well, I went for his shoulder first, and then—"

"He is lying to save me, Justin," said Sophie, as she
opened the door and came out into the yard, her head
held high, in spite of her tangled curls and muddy,
creased attire. "I hit him from behind. He fell like a

stone, Hal said his neck was broken."

"It certainly is," agreed Justin, his eyes softening in sympathy as he saw her bruised face and shadowed eyes. "Are you harmed?"

"Bruised in mind and body," she replied curtly.

"That's why I was trying to save you the trouble of having to testify," sighed Hal, unable to summon the energy to dispute with them.

"You'd never have got your story straight," said Justin. "You've a fever by the look of you." He laid his cool dry hand on Hal's forehead. "I think our priority must be to get you both back to Chawcester."

"A fever? I thought it a hangover," said Hal, amazement in his voice and some relief, for he'd been feeling increasingly foolish at his inability to control his body. "The wine Durward had was strong, and I'd had nothing to eat since yesterday breakfast."

"I've my noon-piece with me, if you'd care for that, your honour," said the constable, overhearing as he'd been hovering. Ned, who had found the young horse, was examining it with care.

"An excellent idea!" Hal was suddenly feeling light-headed with relief. "Sophie, come break your fast, Dogberry here has a feast to set before us."

Justin cast him an anxious look, as the constable, nothing loath, took a napkin from his saddlebag and spread it out on a barrel before them. "'Tis only bread and cheese, your honour," he said shyly. "But my Nan do bake her own bread, and I do tell her, 'tis fit to set before the King of England, I do."

"Indeed it is," said Hal, breaking the crust and passing it to Sophie.

"There's a cow back in that barn, lowing fit to burst, from not having been milked," said the man, eyeing them with simple satisfaction. "Happen the lady would like some milk, to soften the bread?"

"A good idea," said Justin. "Especially if the wine was strong."

"Not only strong, but gone," said Hal laughing, as the gratified constable disappeared into the barn.

"Is he drunk?" Ned asked in an undertone, viewing his brother's flushed cheeks and shining eyes with dismay.

"On the edge of delirium, I think, from loss of blood," said Justin. "We must get him back to Chawcester, and get that wound looked at as quickly as possible, before he goes into a high fever! Is that horse fit to be ridden?"

"No, he's not damaged beyond repair, but he'll not bear any weight for a while," replied Ned. "We'll just have to take them both up before us. If you take Hal— for you are the lighter, and your horse the better—and I take Sophie pillion, then Sambourne can throw the body over the back of his horse. If we take it slowly, we'll get there before noon."

"Come and help me dress Hal, then, for I am most anxious to get him back into Libby's care," agreed Justin.

It was, in fact, afternoon when they finally arrived back at the house in the High Street, and Cecily flew to open the door for them. Her face was as white as Hal's, who'd steadily worsened on the long ride. He was half-lifted, half-carried into the house, and up the steep stairs to the bedchamber. The French physician, summoned by Sambourne, who'd ridden on ahead, once it became clear how ill Hal was, awaited him.

In spite of all the man's great care and Libby's tender nursing, Hal sunk into unconsciousness, and his family waited for an anxious few days, while the whole of the town was abuzz with the scandal of what had occurred.

⚜

Chapter Twenty-Two

It was well into June before Hal was properly back on his feet again. He still didn't look in health, the flesh having melted from his bones in the fever, and dark shadows still marked his eyes towards the end of each day. But it was more in his spirits that the greatest change was obvious, for if he'd been low before the fever, he was morose now, barely opening his mouth unless addressed directly, and seeming to find too much effort in even the simplest conversations. They all tip-toed round him, anxious not to irk him, and Libby spoke hopefully of a full return to health once they were back at Westwood. Justin, however, had his doubts and finally decided he could wait no longer to discuss certain matters with his brother-in-law.

For a while, they chatted in the best bedchamber, overlooking the busy High Street, where Hal, resplendent in a silk bed-gown, spent each morning with books and writing implements. Justin noted his air of contentment with the house, and remarked upon its fate.

"Sophie has given instructions for me to sell this house, you know, Hal," he said, as Hal sat quietly looking out on the busy scene, visible through the leaded panes of the big window. "It seems friend Capel is like to be interested."

"Capel the attorney?" asked Hal. He made a face. "I shouldn't be in any hurry. Like as not, Sophie will change her mind, I'll talk to her about it. This is a fine old house. I'd not like to think of it getting into Capel's hands."

"She seemed pretty determined," said Justin. "She said she'd never be able to forget what had happened here."

"Most old houses have a chequered past," said Hal in dismissive tones. "Tell Capel we aren't selling. I don't know what ails you, to be indulging a female's whims like this. Once Sophie is over the shock, she'll feel differently. This is the only house she's ever known, she'd be sorry if we allowed her to abandon it. But don't fret, I'll discuss it with her."

"She's—she's—erhm—she's left Chawcester, Hal,"

said Justin. He was surprised at how nervous he felt at disclosing this news. "The gossip was rather nasty, you know, and she'd none here she cared to see. So I—I sent her back to Westwood, with Ned and Cecily last week, when you were still so ill."

Hal continued to look out of the window, but a slow anger was building up inside him. "Why?" he asked evenly.

"Well, as I said, she felt a measure of dismay at meeting people. Everyone knew she had been abducted by Durward, and held by him for some hours. There was much speculation and discussion about her killing him, and—and, well, everything really!"

"And you wanted her out of the way," Hal said in the same light tone.

"And, I wanted her out of the way," Justin agreed after a pause.

Hal turned to look at him, his face grim, his eyes hard, like pebbles. "Are you so convinced of your superiority, you cannot trust me to order my own affairs?" he asked in a light, biting tone.

Justin reddened, and kept a rein on his own temper, hoping to avert a quarrel by making Hal see the humour of it. "Well, you appeared to be in some trouble, the last time we were together," he remarked, with a half grin.

"On the contrary, I had arranged matters," Hal replied, refusing to be amused. "I do believe we've had this discussion before, Justin, and I don't know how to make myself plain without being offensive any longer, so understand this: I shall attend to my own affairs, which are not—and never shall be—any concern of yours."

"My sister's happiness must—and always will—be my concern," Justin retorted quickly.

"Your sister has been my wife these past five years, she is no longer your concern, but mine! If and when she makes complaint, you may—and I say may—feel there are grounds for discussing my affairs. Until that date, I would ask you to keep entirely to your own business."

"Sophia Redcroft is my business, I am also named her guardian," snapped Justin, his eyes dark and angry in the face of so direct a snub.

"I fail to see any connection," Hal returned loftily.

"Oh don't you!" cried Justin, incensed. "Just because you've been in a fever these past ten days, it doesn't mean all hell hasn't been let loose here! Rumour and speculation are rife, Hal! Gossip abounds! Do you think any

of these worthy citizens don't know how the Justice gal-
loped off on a half-broken filly, to rescue Sophie from
a manic murderer, and then got himself half-killed in a
duel and spent the night immured in a farmhouse with
her!"

Hal went white. "That is an absurd parody of what
actually happened!" he cried, outraged.

"And current coinage!" Justin snapped. "How do you
think my sister likes to go amongst folk—each and every one who has this story off by heart? Do you think
for one moment the constable didn't see Sophie in her
petticoats and tell a tale of what had been going on in
that lonely farmhouse?"

"I was injured!" Hal cried furiously. "Even he could
see that."

"Aye, and drunk too, or so it seemed," retorted Justin.
"A famous story that made in the telling! The drunken
Justice, who sat in judgement on them the previous
week, at a Bacchanalia the night of Edmund Benton's
funeral with his ward! Now do you wonder I sent her
away?"

"Enough!" Hal cried, getting hastily to his feet. He
strode about the chamber for a few moments, turning
this over in his mind, his fury only further increased.

"And you?" he turned suddenly upon his brother-in-law. "What do you believe, Justin?"

"I haven't heard your part of the tale, you were too ill to talk," he replied instantly. "But I'm prepared to listen."

Hal leaned back against a bedpost and fixed his brother-in-law with a steely gaze. "I see. So, in fact, you have no innate faith in me. You cannot believe in the best, you must wait to have my word upon it, is that so?"

"Yes," replied Justin nettled. "I've seen how you look at that girl, I've seen how she throws herself at you. I am not a fool, I can imagine the temptation, but if you give me your word that this is all idle lies and speculation, then I shall believe you!"

"I'll see you in Hell first!" cried Hal, in a voice of ice. "I am not some petty clerk awaiting my preferment! I am Sir Henry Westwood, I need answer to no man!"

"No man, but God, and perhaps your wife!" cried Justin angrily.

"I need not answer to God, he sees me!" thundered Hal. "And as for Libby, let her ask me if she wishes!"

"If she dares, you mean!" cried Justin, incensed at his arrogance.

"If she has as little faith as you, yes," he replied. "Now,

pray excuse me, I find I am weary, and would rest my aching head."

"You haven't answered my question!" Justin cried, forgetting now in his anger all earlier thought of caution. "What is to become of Sophie? You cannot be thinking of keeping your wife and your mistress in the same house!"

Hal looked for a moment as if he might hit him, but he visibly checked himself, and strode to the door, opening it. "Go!" he said starkly. "You have insulted me in every fashion possible! I never wish to see your face again, and to aid you in this, please note: I shall not be returning to Westwood Hall. I shall be travelling to France with Phillipe Douay, to seek my father's grave, and assist him in various matters pertaining to his exile."

"France!" Justin cried aghast. "Douay—but—but does Libby know of this?"

"I shall take the earliest opportunity to discuss the matter with her, although, of course, I know it won't be necessary, as you will immediately tell her anyway."

"Discuss the matter? Does she have any choice?" Justin shouted angrily.

"None," Hal replied implacably. "It can only be a relief to her, I imagine, to be rid of me."

"And when will you return?" demanded Justin.

Hal shrugged. "When I am ready."

"And your affairs here, your lands, your children?" Justin was bewildered.

"You can attend to them, you are my legal advisor, and as you never fail to make plain, so much more capable than I! I give you carte blanche do what you will, I care not, only go!"

"Look, Hal, I may have spoken out of turn, in my anxiety and desire for Libby's concerns," Justin began, really taken aback. "You cannot mean—"

"I have asked you to go. I have told you to go. Now I command you to leave me be! My next resort must be to physical violence, and with your exquisite care for my health, I'm sure you'd not want me to attempt that!" Hal shouted, advancing on him with real menace.

Justin decided the better part of valour was discretion, and hastily left the room. Hal sank back into his chair by the window. He was amazed at the fury, which possessed him in equal parts with sheer physical weakness. He sat so for some ten minutes, never moving, not even when the door opened again, and the soft silk of Libby's gown hushed over the polished floorboards to herald her arrival.

"Is it true?" she asked starkly.

"Is what true?" he replied, his voice cold and re-
mote.

"You are leaving for France with Doctor Douay?" she
asked, her words seeming to choke her.

"Yes," he replied. He turned to look at her. "You don't
ask—like your impudent brother—if Sophie is my mistress, I note."

"No," she replied. "I don't. I know you."

His hard, insolent gaze fell, and weak tears filled his
eyes. "Thank you," he said curtly.

"So, why do you go?" she asked, hope entering her
voice, advancing a few steps.

He looked down at his hands. "I—I think it may be
for the best," he said quietly, all anger fled now, leaving
him looking stark and ill. "I have felt a need for some
months now to—to come to terms with my father. I
want to—to see his last resting place. And I do not want
to be at Westwood." This last was spoken very quietly.

"I am sorry to drive you from your home. I can send
Sophie to Mary or Bess, if it would be better," she said,
trying to keep the desperate appeal from her voice, but
determined they should understand each other.

"No, it wouldn't be better," he said, his tone bitter. "It would be just the same. Truly, Libby, I am best away from you all for a while."

"It—it seems very hard—on—on the children," she said, her voice clogged with tears.

"I'll return as soon as I may," he replied, his own words unsteady. "You must kiss them both each night for me, and have them remember me in their prayers."

"You are not even coming back first?" she asked, appalled, as the truth was tacitly agreed between them, and could hardly believe what was happening.

"No, no," he said quickly. "Believe me, Libby, believe me, 'tis better this way."

"Better for whom?" she whispered, tears filling her eyes, her voice breaking, she could no longer deny the hold this girl had on him. "Better for me? For little Harry? For my sweet baby?"

"Libby," he said starkly. "I know I injure you, and I am sorry for it, but if you'd not have me injure you more, let me be."

"What must I do, Hal, go down on my knees and beg?" Her tears were falling in earnest now, as she suited her actions to her words. She was desperately afraid if she let him go now, she'd never get him back again.

He'd become the stranger he was when they first married, and if she didn't bridge the distance which had suddenly opened up between them, she'd lose him forever. "I am not proud, I never have been, all I am is a reflection of you, without you, there is no me!"

He put his hand over his eyes to blot out the sight of her beseeching face, desperately trying to equate his sense of justice and duty with the inner turmoil he suffered. If only they'd let him be for a few weeks. If only they'd give him time to quietly come to terms with his own feelings, perhaps then, he could carry on, but in the face of her distress, he was forced to give way. "If you are so distraught, then plainly, I must think again."

"Oh, Hal, do you mean it?" she staggered to her feet, catching her heel in her gown, so that she almost fell into his arms. He held her off, helping her to her feet.

"Yes," he said curtly. "I mean it. If it's going to cause so much disruption and dismay, I'll have to find another way. I'll have to return to my position, but please Libby, give me a little peace, my head is aching fit to burst, and I am so weary I can hardly stand."

"You must go to bed immediately," she said, all concern. "I'll make you a tisane and—"

"No!" he cried, thinking of the tisane that Sophie

had brought him which had proved so effective a love potion. "No, I want nothing, just sleep."

"Let me help you to bed then," she insisted. "I cannot bear to think of you in pain. Are you sure—"

"I am certain I need only sleep," he replied firmly, casting aside his gown, and throwing back the coverlets.

She tucked the sheets firmly about him, and patted his hand much as she would have done little Harry's. "You rest now, Hal," she soothed, her relief that he wasn't leaving her echoing joyously in her voice. "Everything will seem so much better when you've slept."

⚜

Chapter Twenty-Three

Libby stood in the window, much as Hal had done the previous Tuesday, looking down over the busy High Street, but seeing nothing.

"I thought you said he'd promised not to go?" Justin said, trying to keep the incredulity and fury out of his voice.

"No, he didn't promise," she replied, her face strained, and as ever, she was scrupulously honest. "He merely said if I were so distressed over his going, he'd have to think again."

"Aye, but that was when he was too weak to leave," exclaimed Justin, his anger boiling over. "And as a result of his prolonged thinking, he went anyway, without a word to anyone. I'd never have believed it of him!"

"I should never have asked it of him," she returned quietly. "I could see he was hard-pressed by all his problems, and in great distress of mind. I should not have tried to keep him. T'was plain he felt trapped."

"Hard pressed be damned!" he cried angrily, as a single tear slid down her chalk-white cheek, and he felt a measure of guilt that his demands on her husband might had contributed to his flight.

"Anyone would think he was the first man to have fallen for a pretty face he couldn't have! I don't know how many men have endured such a state of things, still do, for all I know. But Hal, he needs must make a song and dance of it, and take himself off abroad in this damned theatrical manner! And to France, of all places!"

"Well, you know, he has not been happy in his mind since the reports came through of his father's death," she began, her tone excusing. "It must be hard to be a long way distant, when one's parent dies."

"And hear of it third hand?" Justin demanded, incensed. "Aye, 'tis damned hard, I recollect the circumstance well!"

"Yes Justin, but you were able to talk to me eventually! You could have come in time perhaps, if only you'd not been so very stubborn! Hal must travel to a foreign land for information, I am sure in my mind that is the main reason for his going. That—and to assist Doctor Douay in his desire to clear his name so that he can return from exile."

"Well, you believe that, if it makes you happier," replied Justin roughly. "But I know better, though surely that is an odd friendship."

"It seems very sudden, does it not?" agreed Libby, her voice unhappy. "I mean, I know Doctor Douay had called every day since Hal was wounded and spent at least an hour talking with him. But to—to go off together like that, without a word to anyone? For Monsieur Douay to abandon all his patients, and just up and leave? It has caused such gossip and speculation!"

"Yes," said Justin, and he folded his lips over further words. He'd not been able to conceal a certain jealously of the foreign doctor, who had so neatly stepped, it seemed, into his shoes, to become Hal's friend and confidante. Once, he and Hal had been close enough to spend hours talking, but his accusations had closed forever the door on that friendship. They'd never sit in comfortable companionship again. He found he missed him, missed him horribly, but, that being the case, how much more miserable must Libby be feeling? "Well, what can't be cured must be endured," he said in calmer tones. "At least we shall be at home tomorrow."

"Yes, I hope never to set foot in Chawcester again," replied Libby.

"That's what Hal kept saying, poor devil! He did try every way to escape the little hussy's clutches," Justin remarked, recollecting his friend's efforts to escape earlier.

"She's not a little hussy, Justin," said Libby, with her innate honesty. "She's a poor, misguided child, who has had much to endure these past few months."

"You do have your own way of seeing things, don't you?" he cried in amused exasperation. "If neither Hal nor Sophie is the villain, who the hell is?"

Her eyes reproached him for his intemperate language. "I thought the depositions Hal and Sophie made were clear. Giles Durward," she replied primly.

"Oh yes, he's the murderer," agreed Justin impatiently. "But there's been wider mischief than that, even, in this affair," his voice echoed his dissatisfaction.

"Indeed," she agreed. "Perhaps Master Benton himself was at fault. If he'd left well enough alone, none of those people may have died."

"Robin Tripp certainly did," said Justin hastily, his feelings still raw from Hal's earlier accusations that his interference had lost four innocent people their lives. "Durward's man confessed to setting the other fire, which caused the smoke. He said he didn't know what Giles intended, but once he was implicated, he had to keep on helping, or Giles had threatened to accuse him! Anyway, Libby, I had this dispute with Hal. We are not fit to judge, we can only seek the truth, and the truth shall set us free."

"I don't always want to know the truth," she replied dully, thinking of the long summer days ahead, without her husband. "I think the truth is overrated. I'd prefer a little common ignorance, personally. I think I'd be happier if I'd never known of all this."

Justin looked appalled. "But that strikes at the foundation of our existence," he cried desperately. "You are saying ignorance is bliss."

"Were Adam and Eve not blissful, in their ignorance in the Garden of Eden?" she returned. "Do you truly think they were happier cast out of the Garden to fend for themselves?"

"Yes, yes!" he cried passionately. "They were like innocent children, they had to grow up, to learn to live their own lives."

She sighed, her thoughts distracted from the philosophical to the purely practical. "As do all children. What shall I tell little Harry?"

"He'll manage," soothed Justin. "And I know Hal, he won't be long gone. He loves England and was too long in exile to remain away for very long. You'll see, he'll be back home in no time."

"And in the meantime, what do we do with Sophie?" she replied.

❧ THE END ❧

Enjoy the

First Chapter

of the next book in the series:

"Calling the Kettle Black"

which begins on page 310

The Last Chapter
of the previous book:
"A Trip to Jericho"

Ned bounced cheerfully into the Hall the next morning, his ruddy cheeks flushed with exercise, a broad smile on his freckled face.

"Father has gone then," he announced.

All eyes turned on him at once.

"Father? Gone?" Hal cried incredulously.

"Gone? I had thought them both still abed," said Libby, in dismay.

"Indeed," Mary replied tartly. "I can't imagine Jacqueline leaving her bed much before noon."

Ned looked adoringly at Cecily as he took a seat opposite her, then he grinned again. "Jacqueline was spitting fury and that woman of hers, Marie, was as sullen as a winter's day—but there they all were in the stables, at five o'clock this morn when I went to saddle up a horse to take out my hounds. Which reminds me, Hal, there's a vixen in cub over at—"

"Oh, never mind your hunting, Ned!" Bess interrupted impatiently. "Tell us do! What did father say? Why, if he has left us Hetta can't be married!"

"Aunt Margery and Aunt Kate are due back tomorrow. They'll be so cross, for Cousin Tom can ill-spare them at the moment," cried Mary.

"Most of what father was saying isn't repeatable," said Ned. "His horse had thrown a shoe and he was forced to travel in the coach with Jacqueline, which plainly wasn't part of his plan. He said the King had recalled him, and that they were for France."

"Don't fret, Hetta," soothed Hal, as she and Will looked at each other in dismay. "Father told Libby the same tale last night. It seems I am to give you away as was planned earlier. There will be no need to cancel the wedding."

All the women immediately relaxed, as Hetta replied prettily: "I'd sooner it was you anyway, Hal."

"When you say 'tale' Hal, is one to assume you are not convinced by it?" Justin asked, frowning.

Hal smiled grimly. "It sounded a little thin to my mind, Justin. It had been my intention to discuss the matter further this morning. I know I should have pursued it last night—late as it was—but I must confess by the time Carver, Jane and I had settled that monstrous husband of hers into bed, I was sore weary and not in need of another quarrel."

"You thought there would be a quarrel?" asked Mary doubtfully.

"Jacqueline seems determined on most occasions to promote one," replied Hal wearily.

"I've never known a female like your stepmother, Hal," agreed Guy. "She's nothing but trouble, that woman. I tell you what, we're better off without her."

There was a pause as everyone, who had previously been considering the state of their affairs and wandering what could be done, thought about Guy's statement.

"Certainly Aunt Margery and Aunt Kate will be happier if Jacqueline is no longer one of our number," said Hal, who'd been dreading explaining all the shocking events to his aunts.

"Yes, you and Libby must be greatly relieved, too," said Mary tactlessly.

"I don't think anyone of us will miss Jacqueline's unkind remarks," said Bess quickly. "And if Hetta's wedding can go ahead after all, perhaps Jacqueline and Father's departure is for the best."

"At least Jacqueline won't be here to recount the more recent events with great relish to our wedding guests," said Libby with an inward shudder, as she thought of how it might have been.

All around the table brightened visibly. "Indeed," said Justin thoughtfully. "Once our stepmother's funeral is over later today, Libby, there should be no further occasion to discuss the matter."

"Hughes said last evening at his departure, that he thought his report would take a few days before becoming common knowledge," remarked Hal.

"So we can easily pass it off as a tragic accident for now," said Mary. Then as they all looked askance at her, she added sharply: "Well, we can, you know! Oh, yes, there will be talk, it's true, but if we just try to remember that it was a sad accident by one who didn't know the house, I think we might get by. After all," she added as Hal opened his mouth to dispute this, "we don't want to ruin Hetta's wedding, do we?"

"No!" agreed Hetta, Will, Libby, Bess and Cecily in unison.

"All we want to do, Hal," said Mary sweetly as he fell silent, "is to stand firm as a family and that is something we Westwoods are very good at!" ❧ THE END ❧

Enjoy the First Chapter of the next book in the series:

Chapter One

Late November
1665

Hal rode slowly up the avenue to the house. The frost had coated everything overnight with a powdering of white. Every blade of grass, every branch, every twig stood out in stark clarity from the blackness of its background. It was well past noon, but still the country was gripped by the thrall of cold and ice. Hal felt it had entered his soul, numbing his heart, so that it physically hurt him.

Never had Westwood looked so forbidding as on this November afternoon when already the light was fading. His horse, weary and despondent, taking its cue from its master, faltered as the great balk of the house robbed the sky of the last brightness. It loomed over them like an ill-omened bird of prey.

The door was closed and the windows shuttered, but as he came to a halt outside, the door opened and a servant, garbed in new black clothes, scuttled forth.

"Welcome home, Sir Henry," he said. "Though 'tis an ill welcome we give you."

"Thank you, Thomas," Hal dismounted heavily, his voice sounding odd and cracked from disuse.

"Mistress Jane be inside, sir," he said, leading the horse away.

Hal straightened up as if shouldering an intolerable burden, and having quickly scanned the façade of his home from dull eyes, he pushed open the door into the hallway.

A fire smouldered in the hearth flanked by two upright chairs. On one of these sat his sister, her strawberry-blonde hair covered with a cap. She rose to her feet, her face pale and her grey eyes shaded by grief, yet filled with sympathy. She smiled a sweet smile. "Hal," Jane said softly. "How glad I am that you are come."

"Even if I am too late?" he added, his voice harsh.

She pressed his arm with her slender fingers. "I have no doubt you came as soon as you were able, you obviously got the note I sent to the inn in Dover," she replied calmly.

He sighed heavily. "It was waiting for me. When was the funeral?"

"Tuesday," she said, her voice almost a whisper. "We waited as long as we could but with no word from you, no knowledge of where you were—"

"You don't have to reproach me," he interrupted. "You cannot do so more than I do myself."

"I do not reproach you, Hal," she replied with calm dignity. "I know you well enough to know you have an active conscience. You need reproaches from none."

"Tell that to Justin, to Mary," he replied bitterly.

"Justin is bound to take the death of his sister hard," said Jane reasonably. "Mary, too, was very fond of Libby."

"And you were not?" he asked sharply.

"I, like you, loved her dearly," she replied. "But to reproach you for something not your fault won't bring her back."

He turned and hugged her close in mute thanks for her confidence. She felt how tense he held himself, how he seemed to tremble with sheer fatigue and grief.

"How long have you been travelling?" she asked.

"Over a week, near enough," he replied. "The Loire was in flood I had to travel miles to get a crossing. I thought I'd never get here."

"Well you are here now," she said in a soothing manner. "Come into the parlour and I'll mull you some wine."

She led the way into the small parlour where a fire burned brightly, shining on the polished panelling. He took a chair by the blaze as she went to get the wine, extending his icy limbs to the flames. As the heat of it began to melt his hands and feet, so did the great lump of ice that was his heart. Tears slid weakly down his cheeks and dropped unheeded into his cravat. Jane, entering with a jug of fragrant spiced wine and a savoury stew, made no mention of it and gave no sign, merely putting the dish of food to keep warm and giving a mug of wine into his unresisting hand. He drank deeply several times and was heartened by it so that he was able to control his grief enough for her to give him the bowl of stew.

"Eat this, Hal," she said kindly. "Then I think you should sleep."

"Sleep?" he replied hollowly. "There's been no sleep for me."

"So I guessed, looking at you," she replied compassionately. "But you are home now, safe, you'll sleep."

He took a few mouthfuls of the stew. "Where is everybody?" he said, suddenly puzzled at the quiet of the house.

"Mary took the children to Elmley Park," she replied, for the first time her gaze faltering. "Libby insisted on it before she—when, well she said she—before it happened. Bess and her babies are with Justin in Adamsholme. Ned and Cecily have gone to Rushington Manor, and Ambrose is with them," she added uneasily.

The combination of the warmth, the strong wine laced with herbs and the food were having their inevitable effect. Hal's head was nodding as he struggled with consciousness. "Hetta? Hetta and Will?" he asked desperately.

"They are well," agreed Jane, removing the empty mug from his slackened grip. "Come Hal, come to bed, you are exhausted."

Leaden-footed he followed her up the shallow staircase off the hall, to the gallery above. Everywhere was dim, warm and above all, comforting in its familiarity. He opened the door to the left at the head of the stairs and almost staggered to the high bed hung about with curtains. He fell across it, and the last thing he remembered was his boots being removed and a cover being smoothed over him with gentle compassionate hands.

When he awoke, it was full daylight and he just caught the sound of a softly shutting door. He sat up

abruptly, realising that he'd slept long and scrambled
from the bed. The fire had been re-made and was burning brightly. Two pewter ewers stood, one filled with
hot water, the other with cold, beside a basin with his
razors laid out ready for him.

Unseen hands had also unpacked his clothes and
washed and pressed his linen. He drank deeply of the
cold water, and then poured the remainder over his
head before shaving himself.

Some time later, feeling comfortable and more
like his usual self then he had since he left France, he
opened the door and stepped out into the corridor. To
his right, the stairs led down to the hall where he could
hear voices, opposite was the chamber which had been
Libby's. He crossed to it and opened the door. All stood
silent, no fire in the hearth, but the bed made up fresh
and her things yet still there. He stood before the toilet
table, fingering the milky pearls, which had been her
favourite ornament and her reflections seemed to look
back at him from the fine Venetian mirror, quizzical, a
little dismayed, but infinitely comforting. He felt tears
prickle the back of his eyes, but controlled them, going
to the closet. Here, all her gowns were hung along with
her thick fur cloak. He lifted a sleeve and held it to his

mouth, inhaling the smell, and then turned abruptly, closing the door and walking swiftly from the room.

The sound of voices came from below and he easily recognised those of Ned, his brother, and Ambrose Carver, Jane's betrothed. Quickly, he descended the staircase.